THE DEVIL'S A HUNTING

Book three

P and K Stoker

Amazon

To our lovely friends xx

CONTENTS

THE DEVIL'S A HUNTING

CHAPTER ONE

Harry and Bub's apartment was crowded with the groaning and injured, but chuft adventurers…

"Did we manage to get everyone home? Do we need to do a headcount or a crocodile holding hands sort of thingy?" Harry was assured that everyone that should be in Hell number one was, in fact, present. Plus, they all felt that they'd dealt with enough wrinkly skinned creatures to last them until a fortnight next Tuesday.

"Well, I think it's fair to say that I've had more than my fair share of adventures for the moment. Even my toenails hurt. A lot. I haven't done any tap dancing for years and now I remember why. Oh, how I remember why. I will never again complain about being left behind to 'mind the shop.' No, I'm quite happy here with my colour-coded clipboards, memos, and free vending machine access. I'll give the gore and viscera a wide body swerve for now on. Thank you very much." Karen was tentatively cleaning her head wound as she eased herself, with a sigh, onto the soft corner sofa.

Her stunning Wickedly Evil Stepmother costume was in absolute tatters. It was covered in fine grey dust, chunks of stage setting debris, fragments of broken bone and lumpy congealed blood clots. She had so wanted to wear that outfit again, and she knew that Dr Riel had also wanted her to wear it again. He was really quite insistent that she wear it again. Oh, that naughty man and his need to play doctors and awfully misbehaving patients. On a more positive note: not all of the blood on her outfit was her own. She also knew the tiny slivers of bone belonged to a particularly vicious Knight. A Knight who would think twice before pointing his accusing finger at a bruised and exhausted artist.

"You have free vending machine access? When did you sneak that one in? Eh, how did you manage that? What a fudging liberty? That just isn't cricket. Could even be favouritism? Or maybe cronyism? Or just...other isms? Can I have an ism too?" Devil Keith had basked in his glory as hero of the hour and saviour of the masses. Well savour of Harry's sisters and the trapped Hell number three Knights. He was now ready to start cashing in on all his fame and fortune. He had decided that he needed to see his mate Alan, as quickly as possible, as he now had yet more items that required designing and printing.

Devil Keith thought he'd start with tee-shirts, scarves and mittens with slogans referring to his role as Hell number three's dastardly conspirator and spy. Plus, he decided that he'd use some glorious catchphrases referring to his pivotal role in finding the real Hell number three conspirator and spy. Although, in some twisted form of logic he still maintained that he was, in fact, the aforementioned conspirator. Last but not least, he required promotional material with slogans about his heroic acts in saving Willing, Fachance and the Hell number three Knights.

Devil Keith daydreamed about a massive celebratory parade, a winding sea of festive floats, bursting fireworks, wood nymphs a frolicking and many, many scantily clad dancing girls. He really did have a thing about parades and ticker tape. The fact that he could retain that request told Harry how serious he was about his need, aka incessant demands for said parade. Harry had Devil Keith's colossal parade and a visit to Kilimanjaro to scatter the ashes of his jeans on her *"to do"* list. These two activities sat right next to her regular optician appointments and her monthly de-lousing session. Being the Horsewoman of Pestilence had its drawbacks.

However, before the parade and all that intrusive confetti Devil Keith believed that first he had to get his hands on the fudging vending machine passes. He decided that was a crucial security requirement and Angel Gab would back him up on that conclusion. How he reached that fanciful assumption was anyone's guess.

"*That's what you took from all my comments? Really? No concern for my general wellbeing or my crushed feet? You really are something else. And before you ask, that wasn't a compliment. Anyway, I'm quite certain that you'd bankrupt Hell number one within the week if you had a pass, Devil Keith. So no, you can't have a free vending machine pass. Plus, if you get one then everyone would be entitled to one.*" Karen's pounding headache had removed all attempts at diplomacy. She was a bundle of aches and pains that desperately needed a long cuddle, a shortbread finger and some warming Horlicks.

"*What do you mean everyone would be 'entitled'? Everyone? Fudge that. Are you forgetting that I am unique and the only one deserving of a free pass? I saved the mission, and it's not the first time that I've been totally indispensable during one of these escapades. I'd go as far as to say that it was now a habit. In fact, I demand you hand over your pass.... you mere woman.*" Devil Keith cocked his pierced eyebrow and ran his hands down his magenta, velvet smoking jacket.

"*Devil Keith, before you say any more. Ponder on this. I have a splitting headache, my feet are sore, I'm bleeding all over my lovely new outfit and I'm tired. Need I say more?*" Karen shuffled forward on her soft cushion and made to rise from the deep, comfortable sofa. Her intention to do him harm was very clear: even to a guy sporting a red fez, neon yellow culottes and fluffy, lime green mules. His battered Prince Charming armour was now home to a thriving aspidistra plant and his carefully constructed General's uniform was missing; presumed stolen for some nefarious role playing. Well a Four Star General needed healing hands and could misbehave too, according to Dr Riel.

Devil Keith stepped back and pushed Harry in front of him. "*Well, with the correct incentive, I could aim for bankrupting our Hell within the month instead. That sounds good, now doesn't it?"* Devil Keith thought this was a genuine concession as he smiled, expectantly, over Harry's left shoulder. He took a deep, hope filled breath. He was getting ready to excitedly clap his hands then head downstairs to snaffle enough pilchard tea and an extra-large whale blubber coffee so that he could bathe in the fragrant concoction. He then decided, as a treat, he was going to add a coconut sprinkled donut to the mix so that he could play *"sink the Titanic and kill all the survivors",* whilst luxuriating in his baby blue tub.

"Ok. I'll think about it. I'm too tired to do the maths just now. I propose that we nurse our wounds and get a good night's sleep. We have a lot of healing ahead of us, then we have a mountain of work to do." Karen signed and rubbed her blistered feet.

Devil Keith made to argue with her but he was stared down by a particularly brutal mama bear look from both Harry and Karen.

"Do all women come pre-programmed with that scary scowl?" Devil Keith wondered but he didn't quite build up the courage to ask.

CHAPTER TWO

T ime for recovery...

Willing and Fachance were now asleep in Bub's old room. The room was still as battered and several feet smaller than it should be, but to the injured sisters it was pure heaven. Dr Riel had patched them up and was very hopeful regarding their physical recovery. The multicoloured bruising looked mighty sore but most of the underlying fractures had already healed relatively straight. The bones might need re-broken and re-set, but he'd deal with that if and when it was required. The dove bites were more of a concern as they had become seriously infected; down through the soft tissue and into the bone. However, they were now scrubbed clean and had been carefully bandaged. Willing and Fachance had been hydrated and received much needed, simple foodstuffs before being ushered into bed. Fachance had licked the plate clean then scratched into the pattern, so that was a positive sign. Although she remained suspiciously silent throughout the exchange.

Dr Riel was less confident about their mental health recovery as they had both been systematically tortured, torn apart, ridiculed and starved. He feared that they would take some time to regain their self-confidence and their identity as badass motor biker's. He had already booked in a series of counselling sessions to explore their needs, concerns, and trauma recovery. Purely coincidentally, he was so anticipating the urine infused tea that would bring him. He wasn't sure if he should mention that particular trait to Karen. That mama bear stare was scary, in the extreme.

Again, do all women come pre-programmed with that scowl?

CHAPTER THREE

Harry and Bub's apartment...

The rescued Knights were physically frail, but they were also completely furious. The despicable King had enjoyed burning them with the Crab's cigars, breaking their limbs, dislocating their joints and hacking at them with dulled machetes. This was done whilst systematically starving them, so they had little chance of healing from their wounds. They were all glad that the King was currently entrenched in strawberry jelly, at the bottom of the castle's moat and his talentless brother was trapped in Hell number eight. However, it was a bittersweet victory as the Knights were enraged that they hadn't been able to participate in all the fighting. Although, to be fair, they were also extremely grateful that they had escaped with their heads still attached to their bodies. The King had planned a bonanza talent show night with the intention of decapitating the Knights and as many of the Hell number one management team as he could capture. He had other plans for the Horsewomen of the Apocalypse and the Knights had been sickened by the King's fever filled eyes as he described the "*sport*" to be had.

The removal of their head was something that the demon Knights couldn't quite, fully recover from. The Knights had only witnessed it once before and to this day they still spoke about it in hushed tones. Sir Gerald De'Nuisance was the unfortunate Knight in question that had re-grown his head. Although, in all honesty it was more of a misshapen protrusion that resembled a bleached blancmange than an actual functioning head. A blancmange that had been found scrambling under a teenage boy's bed after being rolled in crispy, sport socks and semi-digested chicken korma. So, the Knights were very grateful indeed to still have functioning, attached skulls that would not feature on a dodgy dessert menu!

On that note: Sir Muckle of Nursingerton was still having major issues with his head and the crushed vertebrae that use to be his neck. His left ear was currently resting on his left shoulder, so walking was more complicated than usual for the young chap. He had developed a compensatory hump, a painful limp and a pronounced rasping lisp. He was also dribbling excessively, and his green tunic was soaked through. The strings of thick, dripping saliva meant that he was now struggling to talk. The loss of coherent speech appeared to upset Sir Muckle the most, well that and Devil Keith referring to him as Sir Quasimodo of the Bell. Wherever did Devil Keith get that big brass, church bell from? The one that he was currently happily swinging in front of the unfortunate young guy.

Sir Alan de Aloha lost both his eyeballs during the fighting; one to a dulled spoon and the other to a glittery glass heel. Although, he assured Dr Riel that he had been through worse. The previous week he'd had to seek urgent assistance to have a Russian Dwarf Hamster withdrawn from an intimate area. He failed to mention that he'd lost a rather crucial bet, so he'd been the one to have put it up there in the first place. So, the unscrewing of the heel and the dislodging of the spoon, from the aforementioned eyeballs, was tricky and gruesome but relatively easily.

He whispered to Dr Riel, "*at least it didn't involve three ladles of softened peanut butter, a set of blistering curling tongs and twelve ripe kumquats this time. So that was a definite win for me this week.*"

The shoving back of the eyeballs into his blood-filled sockets was surprisingly simple too. Wet, sloppy, gooey, slurpy and noisy: but still relatively simple. However, Sir Alan still insisted on getting first choice of Dr Riel's prized star stickers as he was, *"a brave little soldier".*

The silently sobbing Sir Fergus of D'Fries was lamenting the loss of his exquisite strawberry blonde hair and it was highly likely that he would be wearing a toupee or a hat for the foreseeable future. Devil Keith had offered him clumps of plaited hair that looked suspiciously like Bub's hair, but Sir Fergus had respectfully declined the offer. Instead, Sir Fergus had chosen a wide-brimmed, straw, beribboned bonnet in its place. It really suited him and his wing mirrors, fitted on either side of the hat, were really quite beautiful. Devil Keith packed him a second bonnet so he could have one of them as a spare or save it as his *"Sunday best."* This seemed to appease Sir Fergus as he was now spending an inordinate amount of time pouting in front of the large bevelled mirror.

CHAPTER FOUR

D evil Keith is not a gracious host...

Devil Keith dragged his feet and grumbled as he reluctantly took the bedraggled Knights to his spacious room. He was mumbling about them getting bloody clumps on his fragile lace and stringy white ligaments all over his polished diamantes. He was also throwing around comments about massive disruptions to his luxury Tuxedo design empire and requiring compensation for the expected damage to his reputation. He conveniently forgot about his role in ruining Chick, the mouse', fashion empire and his refusal to pay compensation to said mouse.

Our Mr Hamhands was absolutely delighted with his recently acquired freedom from Hell number three. And he was positively giddy with his new abode at his friend Devil Keith's apartment. His brass tabletop was tipped at a decidedly sprightly angle, and for the last twenty minutes he had been singing a high pitched warbling rendition of, *"I'm sexy and I know it."* Badly, but still a song is a song is a song: well as far as the portly wee chappie was concerned. His multiple gravity defying pelvis thrusts were surprisingly comely and would come in handy when he went out dating again.

However, things had slightly deteriorated when he'd decided to fist bump members of the Hell team, and he had accidently lodged a startled Dr Riel into the nearest wall. Those hands really are big and strong. He had apologised profusely, then he'd ripped a dazed Dr Riel back out of the crumbling plasterboard. After apologetically and violently dusting off a stupefied Dr Riel, Mr Hamhands had happily toddled off. He had a pocket full of loose change and the need to inspect the tempting vending machines. He really hoped they had a few pounds of square sausage available as he desperately needed to refill his empty cheek pouches.

Angel Gab hadn't stayed for the full de-brief. He'd been rather agitated and flashed off to do something *"most urgent."* The task must have been absolutely essential as the Angel hadn't showered and there were small, killer rubber ducks still tenaciously hanging from his magnificently long dark locks. Dr Riel had helpfully suggested removing the ducks with fresh orange juice, as it's widely known that ducks are deathly afraid of oranges following the introduction and popularisation of the French dish Duck a la Orange. Gab said he'd give it a go; so he collected a net bag of satsumas and a wide tangle comb. Another indication of the urgency of this new mission was that Gab was still wearing the tattered remains of his Faery Godmother outfit rather than changing into his comfortable combat gear and sturdy boots. Although, it has to be said that the corset had coped relatively well with the menacing moat, but his garters and silk stockings were hanging by a veritable thread.

Karen was bone weary following their quest and she left with an equally exhausted, dusty and bemused Dr Riel. The couple held each other up as they slowly shuffled to the office door and off to bed. Dr Riel had worked tirelessly in his need to tend to the wounded and ease their pain. He had also spent most of the previous night and all that day caring for a progressively frail Dippit. He was becoming increasingly worried about her fainting and needed to discuss his concerns with the team.

Whilst the team were away Dippit had frequently flushed green and she was fainting on an increasingly regular basis. She had struggled to follow even the most simple details of their adventure and successes, due to the regular episodes of unconsciousness. Despite their multiple wounds, acute pain and the medical first aid required, the Hell number one team had noticed this worrying development. This needed some urgent and serious attention. Dr Riel had moved this up to the top of the Hell number one *"to do"* list, and he decided that he'd fight Devil Keith or anyone else if they tried to move it back down. Well, his Karen would do all the fighting and he'd do the kissing it all better afterwards.

Stan and Bub took the exhausted, but triumphant Liam and Patrick back home to Ireland. Stan wasn't quite sure how he would explain the adventure to his mammy and da as he didn't want the clever wee mites grounded until they were old age pensioners. However, he was immensely proud of the wee guys so he was concocting a convincing story to cover up the drug use whilst emphasising how great the little ones had done.

The authors request that you don't share this book with Stan's parents...shoosh.

CHAPTER FIVE

Bub and Harry's apartment...

Harry was concerned about the huge bruise forming in the centre of Bub's forehead, so she asked for a closer look at the large purple mound. After a few painful prods she declared, *"Bub, I don't think this is a bruise at all. It's wide at the bottom with a small curve half way up then it comes to a sharpish point at the top. Bub, I don't want to worry you, but I think you have a small horn growing in the centre of your forehead. I think that's why the King's head cracked in two when you hit it. His skull split like an overinflated pumpkin. Wait here, I'll get my medical dictionary, my magnifying glass and some tweezers."* Harry quickly scrambled away and searched for the latest edition of her most favourite book.

Bub checked in the over mantle mirror. He was poking the skin covered lump and wincing. Then poking it again, because that's the most sensible thing to do...right?

"Harry, after dealing with Devil Keith and the Deadly Sin juices, I think I know what this is. I'm pretty sure that I was engulfed in the Deadly Sin of Wrath. When I heard the vicious King say what he had planned for you, I lost it. Yes, I know that he was holding Gab at the time but once he figured out who you really were I knew he was going to enjoy torturing you. He was probably going to be even more vindicative than usual, as he would have felt that he had been fooled by us.

I remember feeling this overwhelming need to annihilate the King. Not hurt him. No, not that. This was the need to completely crush him into dust and remove him from all existence. I could feel my muscles expanding and engorging with blood. My spine began to stretch, and the discs began popping out. I could hear them above my thumping heartbeat. I think they were preparing to change my shape. Preparing me to become a rabid beast.

The rage was frightening, but sorta exciting too. I had no control as I charged at the King. The feeling. It's hard to describe, but suffice to say... it was exhilarating and addictive and all-consuming. I loved it and feared it, all at the time. It was raw power." Bub was still surprised by how fantastic it felt as it energised and motivated him to violence.

"And now?" Harry warily checked. She edged towards the emergency rucksack sitting in the corner of the room. Following Devil Keith's terrifying transformation they had made the decision to keep a *"restraining bag"* in each apartment. The bag contained stainless steel chains, a large iron net, reinforced tent pegs and a large mallet to pound the pegs into the floor. Harry made a mental note to ask Stan if he could make up some pots of the Deadly Sin of Sloth's sedating wax to add to the rucksacks.

"As soon as I knew you were safely out of danger it quietened down. It only lasted a few minutes, but as I said, I sorta liked it. The lack of control was terrifying, but liberating at the same time. I felt as if I could conquer the world. And, oh wow. I wanted to punish everyone for the slightest indiscretion. This sounds crazy but Santa's naughty list went through my head. Only for a second, mind you. But I could totally understand why some children were given coal for Christmas. I wanted them all to have coal.

And to think, that was only a taste of what Devil Keith experienced when he was overwhelmed with the Greed and Fornication Sin juices. I can't thank Stan enough for saving my bro from those feelings. That must have been terrible... and I'm positive that Devil Keith really would have ended us all that day.

I'm sorry to say this, but Gab's right, Harry. We can't go through that again. We need to get this place better organised and start to behave in a more mature manner. This isn't the anger at the one horn rating talking either. We need to change for all our sakes." Bub nodded and decided to start another new "to do" list.

After a few hugs and whispered endearments Harry and Bub settled into their messy but blessedly peaceful apartment. That's not strictly true. They gracelessly slumped onto the bed, fully dressed, and immediately fell asleep.

CHAPTER SIX

Bub finds out that Harry hates mornings...

"Please tell me that's not my alarm clock. Nope, it can't be. It's a nightmare sent to get me. I just got into this bed. There's no way that it's time to get out of it yet." Harry mumbled then pulled her pillow over her head and snuggled further into their cosy bed.

"*Sorry Harry, ma darling. That **is** your alarm clock a calling. Are you really going into work today? I don't want to interfere, but I really don't think you should. You've had a hellava few days and I think you need to spend time with your traumatised sisters. I'm worried about you, and about them.*" Bub had dislodged the pillow and kissed Harry on her freckled nose.

"*Ah, well. About that. I do have something to tell you. I was sacked. Shown the proverbial door. 'Given my books', as the saying goes. I wasn't sure how to tell you, so I was going to pretend to go in today then break it to you later. Are you disappointed in me?*" Harry peeked out from the top of her quilt and wrinkled her nose.

"*Never. I could never be disappointed with you. To be honest, it's a bit of a relief. I thought that you'd never really enjoyed the management trainee post. All those office politics and getting caught in the middle of silly disagreements over who ate whose peach melba yogurt. You only really became excited at the prospect of ordering and arranging your new stationery. Do you know that you giggle when you talk about your 70% polyester suit, polished brown brogues, your American tan tights, and the smell of your faux leather briefcase? Plus, you were positively giddy and so sexy when you used all that management jargon. So, feel free to use that with*

17

me whenever you want, grrrrr." Bub winked and began tickling Harry's sides.

"Oh, blue sky thinking, plan, do, study, act......" giggled Harry.

The grrrr and giggles developed into a full-blown set of growls and groans then they fell asleep in each other's arms. They woke up a few seconds later and agreed that people only fall asleep in each other's arms in books and movies, as in real life it's too bloody hot and uncomfortable to do that.

An hour or so later...

"What's all that noise? Is that banging I can hear? Is there water running somewhere? Where's it coming from? Make it stop. Please make it stop." Harry struggled from a rather pleasant dream, into a very noisy and crunchy reality.

"Stay here. I'll grab my baseball bat. No, Harry, stay there. I'll go look. I'll shout if I need any help," Bub quickly shook of his sleepy grogginess and silently crept to the bathroom door. He slowly pushed the door open. Wincing as it creaked on its rusty hinges. He popped his head and shoulders into the bathroom.

Less than ten seconds later...

"What the hell are you doing here? Get that fudging monster outta here. Out... now. No, no....don't bring the bathtub with you. I said not to bring it. Spit it out. Spit it out before I make you spit it out." Bub backed out of the bathroom, but was hanging around the doorway. There was the sound of smashing mirrors, shattering glass and sloshing water then there was utter silence.

"I saw you in there. Don't bother trying to hide. Come out and don't bother with the shushing. We can both hear you. Out, now." Bub was hitting the baseball bat against the palm of his hand as he threatened the destructive intruder

CHAPTER SEVEN

Still in Bub and Harry's apartment...

Angel Gab slowly exited the sodden bathroom. He looked decidedly guilty and ever so sheepish, as he was followed out by a forty-foot-long damp crocodile. A forty-foot-long crocodile that was munching through a hand basin, the remains of a shower-screen and a full set of stainless-steel mixer taps. The hungry crocodile was leaving a trail of destruction in his wake, as well as a large number of nearly empty shampoo bottles and a couple of mangy looking loofas.

"*What the....*" Harry had joined Bub at the doorway and she was waving a bright red, Wellington boot in the air. The authors aren't entirely sure what use the boot would have been in deterring burglars. Oh, wait... the stomach-churning smell! That smell would definitely have made folks think twice about entering her apartment and staying long enough to rifle through her belongings.

"*Stop. You are frightening him. He is more afraid of you, than you are of him. Just stop a minute and please, please put down that boot. I can explain everything.*" Shouted the flustered Gab as he stood in front of the mildly curious crocodile.

"*Frightening **him**? I don't fudging think so. Go on then, Angel Boy. Explain, and make it a fudging good one. Tell me why bits of our bathroom are currently in our bedroom and, coincidentally, also in the jaws of a vicious crocodile,*" the sarcasm was positively dripping from Harry's pursed lips. The rude interruption and the awful smell from the boot was not providing the honeymoon vibe she had hoped for.

"*I felt so guilty about my part in your recent adventure. I never normally lose my cool, but it happens on quite a regular basis whilst I am in your company, Ginger Girl.*" Gab tried to take the upper hand, but it was never gonna happen. Not with the honeymooners so rudely awakened from their peaceful slumber.

"*Not helping your case, Angel Boy. But pray continue.*" Harry was stretching, yawning, and scratching her pert bottom. Whilst keeping the repulsive boot as far away from her person as was humanly possible. It was at times like these that Harry wished she looked less like the short-armed T-rex than she currently did.

"*Well after fighting with Roberto. Oh, that is the delightful chap's name. I was full of utter remorse. I normally help people and animals. It is my job and I enjoy it immensely.*

Well, I went to see Duke as I have a standing, weekly appointment with the depressed Kelpie. I was working through his Mindfulness exercises, and I must say he is making steady progress. It was then that I realised that I was no better than Devil Keith and that rotter Jonathan. However, instead of hurtful words I had beaten a poor, defenceless creature into submission. Roberto may be a minor demon, but he has feelings just like everyone else.

I then went back to check on his wellbeing. I found him to be desolate and despondent following his defeat. You will have heard of crocodile tears? Well, these were real tears. He was bawling his eyes out. He had already been struggling with the anti-hypnosis contact lenses and the snug swimming goggles. King Adrian had ensured that those were issued as mandatory crocodile apparel. This mandate occurred as a direct result of your previous adventures in Hell number three. You really have no idea of how your actions impact on others. Do you?

Also, I am not sure if you are aware of this, but it is no easy task to insert the lenses as Roberto does not have opposable thumbs. He had to wedge the lenses against a rockface then roll his eyeball into the crevice.

He was also finding that the swimming goggles were overly tight and giving him a fierce headache. It was no wonder he used his herculean tail to sweep me into the King's arms. He was in a shocking state: in immense pain, dealing with impaired vision and having to fulfil his henchman duties for an overbearing bully. I should have considered that before diving into the moat, putting him into a chicken wing wrestling hold and further decimating his fragile confidence.

With this additional information and insight, I reasoned that I had to render Roberto some assistance. I initially transferred him to the Falkirk canals to be nearer to Kelpie Duke so that they could both have some much-needed company. Young Baron isn't the most empathetic Kelpie, so the addition of the buddy system would have been good for both Duke and Roberto.

However, after observing his maiden journey along the canal, I felt he was at risk from the Falkirk locals. The ladies from the Inches, in Larbert, do so love their designer handbags. I thought they would yank him out of the canal, as I feared they would be more than willing to endure the risk to their manicures for such a handsome creature.

Do not roll your eyes. He is very handsome and a valuable member of society.

Also, do you know that the local fish and chip shops will batter and fry any edible item? And I do mean any item. A deep fried, battered chunk of handsome crocodile would not have even raised an eyebrow. The locals would have just requested extra vinegar and a pickled egg on the side.

I felt that Roberto had been through enough so I brought him here for some rest and relaxation. He so needs it, the wee scone.

Plus, Bub. I am deeply disappointed in you and your cavalier ways. Roberto asked you to call him and you did not do so. I propose that this is your way of making it up to him.

That is why I am here." Gab smiled and extended his magnificent wings. He was so glad to be back in his Dr Martins and camouflage gear.

"*Sorry...*" Harry stuttered then stared at the crazy Angel.

"*Your heartfelt apology is accepted, Ginger Girl. Let your babysitting commence.*" Gab smiled and pointed at the confused crocodile. The Angel presumed the matter was closed. His job here was done so he made to leave.

"*Excuse me! No apology was given, Angel Boy. I was going to ask you to repeat what you just said as I couldn't believe your gall. So don't bother with the flashing just now. You're staying put until we sort this all out.*

I just can't believe you're trying to pan this off on us. That crocodile is a malicious creature that will eat us as soon as look at us. There's no way we're looking after him. Just no way.

Roberto, stop eating the corner sofa and spit out the microwave, now. I promised that microwave to Brownie Leanne and I don't want to upset her. You don't want to upset her either. Trust me, the Brownies make King Adrian look positively angelic." Harry shuddered and tried to corral the crocodile away from her vulnerable kitchen.

"*How about we negotiate?*" said the hopeful Gab. He surveyed the remains of the room and realised that he may have made a tiny mistake in bringing the hungry crocodile away for a "*break.*"

"*How about you spread those wings a bit further and leave? And take Mr Everso-Chompy with you. Hoy, Roberto, spit that fudging microwave out. Now! I won't tell you again. Do you want a zip added to your tail? Don't you look at me like that. You know what I mean. I will gladly add you to my handbag collection... or Devil Keith's collection. Yeah, when I think about it: more likely Devil Keith's collection. But you will be added. Make no mistake about it.*" Harry stepped towards the chewing creature, and then thought better of it. In the time that she had made her threat the microwave, the slow cooker and the dishwasher were no more.

"*Stop intimidating the poor chap. You have no idea how stressful his existence is. He is a misunderstood, comfort eater. So, how about …a week of sitting duties? Mmmm, Harry? One tiny week? I will even throw in one of those repulsive chicken and pineapple pizza's you like so much. How you can eat that monstrosity is beyond me. Plus, I will add a bottle or two of branded tequila. Tequila with a real worm, rather than the curled up elastic band you normally find at the bottom of one of your economy bottles."* Gab genuinely thought that he was onto a winner with that offer and he smiled accordingly.

"Stop with all the bizarre grinning. It's creepy, and I'm off the tequila. Well Angel Boy, how about … 2 minutes? One minute and 58 seconds…One minute and 57 seconds…" Harry looked pointedly at her kitchen wall clock.

"How about four days of croc sitting and I will owe you a favour? A favour, which I cannot refuse? No matter what you ask of me, I will do it. Well, I draw the line at murder, theft, and arson but anything else. You just have to ask. Oh, and no heists or scrumping either. I have an aversion to apples." Gab screwed up his face at the word apple.

Harry spent all of a tenth of a second considering the offer. *"You will owe me big time, Angel Boy. I will collect. You know I will."* Harry gloated, then she took a big bite out of a rosy red apple. Well, it wasn't all that red as the apple was covered in scrummy toffee.

Gab gulped and slowly nodded. Now he's gone and done it.

CHAPTER EIGHT

S till in Bub and Harry's apartment…

"Well, if we're up then everyone else can get up. Rally the troops, old wifey," and Bub patted Harry's bum. He was clearly a morning person and didn't care who knew it.

"Bub, old husbandie, please. Ten more minutes? Just ten tiny minutes? Eh?" Harry was clearly a tired person and didn't care who knew it. She climbed back into bed and started to snuggle into the soft warm duvet. They had used the remains of the sofa, a side of the washing machine, a seldom used smoothie maker and a three-legged kitchen table to enclose the carnivorous crocodile into a corner of the room.

"How about we check on your sisters and get away from the hungry luggage? Sounds good?." Bub wasn't sure which end was more lethal: the meat slicing teeth or the bone breaking tail of the unwelcome visitor. However, he was sure that he would never forget seeing Roberto eating a stuffed, pink flamingo then burping out the feathers.

"Ok. Ok. If we go now then they might be finished talking by sometime next week. But before we go, can you try to get Roberto to stop eating the radiator? I don't want to have to floss his teeth again. It was really brutal the first and second time I did it. Plus, I'm nearly out of barbed wire." Harry checked her dwindling stash.

"I've always meant to ask. Why do you have a roll of barbed wire at the side of your bed?" queried, Bub.

Harry explained and Bub was really impressed with her logic. In fact, he was so impressed that he decided to put a roll of barbed wire at his side of the bed too.

CHAPTER NINE

B ub's old room...

"Did you sleep ok? Can I get you anything? Anything at all? Painkillers? Some band-Aids? A cuddle? A Tunnock's caramel wafer?" Harry hadn't had a chance to study them the night before, so she was shocked at the condition of her little sisters. She so wanted to wrap them both up in fluffy, cotton wool and hide them from danger. They would immediately slice their way out of the cotton wool and try to stuff it down her throat in order to choke her with it. To be fair, Harry thought that every healthy and loving family would do the same.

"Stop with all the fussing, Harry. It doesn't suit you and it's really making us worry. Bub, what have you done to our Harry? Have you made our big, bad girly into a lily-livered weakling?" Willing was trying to distract Bub and Harry so that she could hide the worse of her injuries beneath the blankets. She had been shocked when she catalogued the number of wounds and severity of their trauma. The King had obviously brought his 'A' game to the torture chamber.

"I wouldn't dare, Willing. We've just been so worried about you both. You've been out of touch for ages. We've been looking for you all over the place. We even put lucky Stan on the case, but even he couldn't do it. Harry and I tried to find you both before the wedding..." Bub was perched at the end of the bed and trying not to move too much in case he jostled the injured women.

"The wedding? Who got married?" Willing and Fachance swapped puzzled looks. Suddenly more awake and extremely interested.

"We did," Harry proudly showed off her wedding and engagement rings. Fluttering her hand in front of their faces then resting it over her heart. She shrugged and smiled. A little embarrassed by the attention, but a lot pleased with the marriage.

"Oh, gorgeous rings, Harry. A bit unusual but they really suit you. Very, very sparkly, and so girly. Took you long enough, Bub....ya, wuss." Willing smiled through the pain and pulled Harry into a half hug. Fachance then pulled Harry into the king-sized bed with them and tucked her in. She was patting Harry's hand, cuddling her in and cooing over the rings.

"Charming as ever, Willing." Bub had forgotten how much he enjoyed talking with Harry's sisters. However, he hadn't realised that they knew that he had previously *"liked"* Harry. He would never have guessed that they were so observant. Although his frequent Devil Keith and Harry rescue missions, plus the regular deliveries of rope were quite a big clue as to his feelings about Harry.

"Charming? Yes, sir. Sure am. Now help us sit up so we can talk like civilised folks. Is it alright if we get more details about the wedding later? We would have loved to have come. I know it's not the same, but it would be nice to have an after-wedding hen night with the four of us. Oh, oh, we could invite Amanda as well. She's so lovely. But only if the hen party idea is ok with you, Harry?" Willing and Fachance sluggishly heaved themselves upright and tentatively checked their cuts and bruises. They were a mess of boo-boos and healing scabs.

"A hen party? Oh, what a great idea. I'd love that. Oiled up men with tiny g-strings? Yum. Bub, it's ok. In the immortal words of the great Sinead O'Connor: 'no one can compare with you.'

Not trying to change the subject... but delaying the wedding chat would be good. Dippit would kill us if we discussed it without her. She can also tell you about her wedding and good news." Harry was quivering with delight.

"What? Really? What the...? Honestly leave you pair alone for

a few weeks and you both get shackled. But seriously: I'm so excited for you both. My big sisters married. Who would have thought it? Next there might be some pattering of tiny feet? Eh, nudge, nudge, Wink, wink. Auntie Willing? I like the sound of that." Willing shivered. She was delighted for them both. Fachance was using her cupped hands to make little hearts in the air.

"Nothing compares 2U," added Bub.

"Oh, that's so sweet. I didn't know you cared." smiled Willing. She gave him a big wink then shoved him off the bed.

"You know that's the song title...Oh never mind." Sighed a mildly exasperated Bub. He knew that Willing was the Horsewoman of War and could cause a hellava fight in an empty house. Although, she wouldn't as she was a bit of a softie at heart and volunteered for every possible charity and rallied for every good cause. However, sometimes it was so hard to *"keep the heid"* and when Willing went *"off"* she really went *"off"*. So Bub just took her gentle ribbing with the good intentions it was intended.

"I can't wait to get all the mushy, slushy details. All the lovely, lovely gossip. Was it a totally dreamy proposal? Chocolates, candlelight, and roses. I bet it was. Bub's loved you from afar for soooo long. He's had that sad, kicked in the face, puppy dog look for simply ages." Willing was positively gooey.

"Have not." Muttered a red-faced Bub as he subtley flexed his muscles.

"Have so. Wait, you can't tell us about all that romance on an empty stomach. Ohh, but it's just so romantic. No, no don't tell me. I can wait. Rightyo, back to the business at hand. But so, so romantic, and cute too.

Now, I must concentrate. First order of business: I think you want to know what happened to us?" Fachance was positively gushing with delight at the prospect of all the pretty wedding details and the cake. Don't ever forget about the cake. It could be the last mistake you will ever make.

"If you're sure that you're able, Fachance. I can wait if you don't feel up to it. You might just want to speak with Harry about it. I could leave." Bub desperately wanted to get away from

his surprisingly observant and embarrassing sisters-in-law. He was not cute. Or a cutie. Or a cutie-pie. He was a red-blooded alpha male who captured his woman and manly dragged her off to his despicable cave. To do even more despicable things to his woman. Afterall, he did have a subscription to *"Knots and Knaughty Monthly"*.

However, Willing and Fachance reasoned that the sooner they started telling people about their ordeal then the sooner they could concentrate on their recovery. Then they could indulge in the details of the weddings (plus cake, the authors aren't forgetting the cake) and plan a hen do or two. And then get them some much needed and certain to be very bloody... revenge.

CHAPTER TEN

S till in Bub's old room...

"*Please stay Bub. It saves us saying it twice. That fudging King Adrian. He did a fair bit of damage, Harry. He didn't let us eat. Not at all. I told him that you couldn't torture people on an empty stomach, but he just laughed. Laughed, I tell you. I then told him he couldn't laugh on an empty stomach so, quick as a flash, he bit off my pinkie finger. I wasn't expecting that. It was mighty nippy. When I accidentally do that to other people do you think it hurts them like that? Ok Harry, you can tell me later.*

Then I told the King that he couldn't be a cannibal on an empty stomach. Next thing I know, Willing is standing over my prone body and I'm two pounds lighter. That King had eaten both my pinkie fingers, my earlobes, my left collar bone, my tongue, my voice-box and both of my thumbs. Luckily, I had been knocked out by then and didn't feel the full effect of the nasty encounter. So, the King had some mercy after all and did the whole cannibal thing while I was unconscious. Not a lot of mercy, but a little bit that helped a lot.

You can just about feel the lump. Funnily enough it's directly on top of my usual head bump," Fachance was softly crying as she recounted that particularly gruesome part of her torture.

Willing was shaking her head and miming knocking Fachance out in order to shut her up. Harry and Bub immediately understood. They knew that Willing always kept a small mallet in her pocket for that type of emergency. Fachance was the Horsewoman of Famine, so she felt it was her duty to ensure that everyone had eaten enough so that they were prepared for any and all tasks the day might throw at them.

The constant over feeding could become a tiny bit tiresome, but Willing had correctly surmised that the King would be less tired and more horrifically delighted at the excuse to slice and dice Fachance even more. So, she had intervened and knocked the troublesome feeder/eater out.

"That skinny King was only wearing an ermine clock. There were no underpants or other essential items of clothing on his personage. It was sickening. Oh, he is so emaciated that I could see the outline of Fachance's collar bone sitting in his shrunken stomach. Being able to see the bone as he digested it: that was the worst part of the torture. Oh, it was so disgusting," shuddered a grimacing Willing. She had a slightly week stomach but tried to soldier on. She also wondered if the King required a Telethon in order to gain funds to bulk out his meagre wardrobe.

"Oh Fachance, you poor wee soul. I'm so glad that your bits have all re-grown, but it must have been so painful. So, so terrible for you both going through that. I'm absolutely fudging furious at him. That King is a certified lunatic. Can I ask? How did the King get to you both?" Harry was rubbing Willing's back and softly kissed Fachance's head bump.

"Still not swearing, Harry? Keeping the sexiness in check...I'm impressed. Having a full stomach will help you stop swearing. I pinkie promise. Oh, just as well they've both grown back.

So, I still have my thumbs to fully re-grow. I can't tell you the rest of our horrific story on an empty stomach and you can't listen to our story on an empty stomach either." Fachance was now attempting to rub her head and her stomach. She thought that would show how difficult it was to multitask on an empty stomach. Harry couldn't take her eyes off the disgusting thumb numbs.

They ate or rather Fachance gorged, and they all watched in fascination and repulsion. Bub was aghast but he couldn't look away. Not at all. How could such a tiny, angelic looking woman pack away two full roast boars and extra crackling? Only the tusks and a particularly hairy piece of skin remained at the side of the platters. The tusks were too difficult to chew through, but Fachance had left a fair few bite marks in her wake. Three dozen soft poached eggs quickly followed the boar. Then there were eighteen flaky croissants complete with whipped cream, soft butter, and lashings of apricot jam. The two pints of fresh lemon curd were eaten straight out of the jars. How could she then ask for a; *"just in case of emergency,"* ready prepared, mid-tale snack? Wow, that woman was a waste disposal unit on legs. You'd be forgiven for saying that you'd rather feed her for a week than a fortnight.

"Ah, all better now. Willing and I went to see Pam. You know Pam. Pam? The motorcyclist that we all know? We met her at that music festival. The festival where Dippit blew all the lights because she had to straighten her hair and cure the common cold? Both at the exact same time. She got so close to the cure too. It's a pity that Dippit has such curly hair and hates it so. Okay, I'm moving on.

The Pam that volunteers to courier blood and grungy human bits around the Highlands? That Pam. You must remember Pam.

Well, we missed her at her lovely, new house but found out she had gone to Orkney to celebrate her birthday. We thought that a visit would be a nice surprise and I so wanted to remind her that she couldn't eat cake on an empty stomach. So, we decided to go see her..." Fachance was slavering at the thought of birthday cake and all those delicious candles.

"Fachance forgot to tell you; that was a couple of months ago." Willing smugly added. She was the organised one of the pair and never, ever forgot to send a thank you note at the end of every lovely visit.

"Willing, that detail's not really needed in this story. You should eat if you're going to interrupt me. You can't interrupt me on an empty stomach. It makes you sound so, so rude." Fachance huffed and began giving her sister dirty looks.

Willing rubbed her mallet.

CHAPTER ELEVEN

S till in Bub's old room…

The authors did warn you that Fachance and Willing could go on a bit, but needing a third chapter to tell a tale that could have been written on the back of a fag (cigarette) packet is bad, even for that meddlesome pair.

"*Ahem, so you were saying?*" Harry had heard many a "*Fachance and Willing tall tale.*" They seemed to go on forever and ever. During a previous story Harry had just cut her toenails at the start of their tale. She then had to cut them again and yet again by the time they had finished. Who tells one story that results in the listener growing and then having to cut their overgrown toenails? Not once, but twice? Twice! Harry was used to trying to speed them up whilst trying to sift out their unnecessary bits of nonsense.

"*Harry, keep your tuffty hair on. It's all very important stuff. Anyway, you've heard of the mystical Selkies? The Scottish beauties? Oooooooooh! Mawhaha,*" Willing attempted a deplorable Vincent Price impersonation. It was predictably terrible, and Harry only knew it was the esteemed Mr Price because Willing told her.

"*Yes.*" Harry quickly confirmed. Keen to keep them on track and away from any further form of impersonation.

"*Eh, no. Can't say as I have.*" Bub received a sharp elbow in the side for that admission.

Harry thought that rather than resorting to brief, but frequent episodes of small acts of violence, she and Bub should develop a secret code so that they could bypass some of Hell number one's more onerous tasks. She quite liked the thought of being called or referring to herself as *"the bride"* or *"your bride"* as a means of drawing Bub aside for a confab. Although she hadn't quite pitched that idea to him yet. The authors predict that would quickly deteriorate to Harry being called *"Frankenstein"*, or *"Frankie"*. As in the Bride of Frankenstein. But they'll keep you posted on that odd development.

"Well for Bub and the solitary reader's sake. The Selkies are also called the seal people, sea people or, on some occasions, mermaids. They're also much nicer than their mermaid cousins. Much nicer. So much nicer. The Selkies are whimsical, gentle, loving, and delicate creatures. Not like those anchor tattooed, fighting monsters that wrestle sharks. Those fighting mermaids would be nicer if they ate more. That's a fact!

Some people think that Selkies are formed from the souls of the drowned, but no one's really sure. I think that's such a lovely idea. A beautiful re-birth into such a mesmerising and beautiful creature.

I don't think I could ever eat a seal. Well, not knowingly. Mmm, maybe just the once: with sticky oyster sauce and paprika Pringles. That would be deliciously salty, crunchy and a little spicy. A well balanced amuse bouche, I think.

You're doing that eye rolling thing again, Harry. I've said it before, and I'll say it again. They'll stay like that.

Anyway, the Selkie are from the Orkney's, Ireland, the Faroe Islands, and Iceland so it was very important that you knew where we had gone and why, Harry. We know you always try to speed Willing and me up. We do get there...we just like to build up some anticipation for our wonderful tales.

I so want to continue, but I now need a teeny totty dish of Eggs Benedict and some toast. Toast slathered in butter, to satisfy part of my itty, bitty hunger. I'm feeling really quite faint. So, I am." With that pronouncement Fachance wolfed down her mid-tale snack of a family sized, casserole dish of eggs and two full loaves of golden toast. Lack of opposable thumbs wasn't slowing this lady down. Not one bit.

Willing enthusiastically took up the tale. "*Fachance you would not eat a seal; I wouldn't let you. They're cute...like Bub over there. Annnd if you did eat one it would be with sour cream Pringles. You know that paprika gives you dreadful wind. I don't want to deal with that again. They keep blaming global warming for the longer hurricane seasons but we both know better. Now don't we, Fachance? It's your colossal bottom burps.*

Okay Harry. Anyway, back to our story. The Selkies are shapeshifters. In water they are sleek seals but on land they shed their skins and become very attractive humans. They're immortal, but can be killed by sharks or humans. Do you think that's why the marauding mermaids wrestle with sharks? An old feud? Mmm, I'll have to look into that. They might need a Benefit or a fund raising Masked Ball.

Humans pose yet another threat: men steal the seal furs so that the Selkies can't go back into the sea. The Selkies are then taken as wives and their skins are securely hidden by their jealous husbands. Selkies seemingly make really good wives and mothers. Who knew?

On the morning after Pam's party, we met a lonely Selkie. She was sitting on a rock, gazing longingly out to sea. Her name was Cesealia. She was in such a terrible state. She so missed the sea and had searched for her skin for many, many years. It was just heart-breaking to hear her life story. It would have brought a tear to a glass eye.

She told us that she had only left the sea for a quick dance on the sand then a tiny bit of sunbathing. She was fed up with only having her top half tanned, so she wanted a bit of overall colour. She was aiming for a mid-brown or possibly a copperish tone. I can show you a colour chart if that would help paint a picture. It would add a bit of colour to the story. Oh Fachance, see what I did there? Paint a picture? Bit of colour to the story?" Willing and Fachance started giggling and doing noisily high-fives. Harry thought they needed to cut back on all their volunteering projects with children and adolescents as it was rotting their brains.

"Please, please get on with it. Bub's gonna need another shave at this rate." Harry pleaded and checked out Bub's stubbly chin.

"You're so impatient, Harry. We don't know how you managed to get such an understanding hunk. Keep your bra on, Harry. We've been injured enough; no need for bra-maggedon. Ha, ha, ha.

Anyway, we decided to help Cesealia to find her skin. Her awful human husband had died before telling her where he hid it. So, with no clues, we searched the north of the island, the south of the island, the east of the island and the west of the island." Willing pointed in the air at an imaginary island.

"Ok we get it: you searched all of the island and...?" Harry was making rolling motions with her hands, but her sister's continued to witter on.

"We couldn't find it. That horrible man had not only stolen her freedom whilst he lived, but he made sure that she couldn't get away even when he died. There was no romance in that marriage. It was so sad." Willing wiped away a small tear.

"That's so grim. The poor, poor seal. Much as it pains me to say this, but what happened next?" Harry began picking the meagre scraps out of the casserole dish. It turns out that you actually can't listen to one of their adventures on an empty stomach. Best not tell Fachance that little gem.

"Well after searching the north of the..." Wiling started with the island again.

"Willing, best get a move on. Harry is fiddling with the wire in her bra again. I don't want stabbed on an empty stomach. Not again." Fachance then grabbed the casserole dish from Harry's lap. She scrutinised it to ensure that she hadn't missed any delectable crumbs. Holding it up to the light she spotted an eighth of an ounce of food that had been hidden by the handle. She twisted and turned until she was able to lick up the speck. Satisfied, she chucked the 1971 Homestead design Pyrex dish over her shoulder, and it smashed into the corner of the room. Bub winced. He feared that his room would never be the same

again. He was planning on setting up his design studio in this room: if he could un-crumple the walls and get the bits back from Devil Keith.

"Ok, Fachance. We stopped for a break. I had just bought my new touring motorcycle. It has a massive 1,854cc air cooled OHV-twin engine. It's high-tech and high-torque, with about 120lb-ft available. Okay, Harry. Let's just say that it's a great bike and I love it. One last thing, it's better than Fachance's bike. Said it and won't take that back, so there." Willing stuck out her tongue and Fachance pretended to grab it. Well Harry hoped that Fachance was just pretending.

"We were on a lonely but beautiful stretch of the road watching the sunset. The colours were stunning. I think I might ask Devil Keith to make me a top in those exact shades. Orange, yellows, and a dash of pink. Yes, I know, Harry. I'll move on.

Well, it suddenly went dark. We quickly realised that someone had put hoods over our heads. The hoods were smelling of blood and vomit, so we thought Devil Keith was playing a prank on us. He is such a terrible scamp. Next thing we knew we were whisked away to a damp, medieval dungeon. We met Sir Daniel..." Willing clarified with a nod.

"Yes Willing, we know the Knights and all of their names." Harry firmly stated.

"Shush, impatient much. Put the bra wire back. So, the King set to work on us. That is our tale. Happy now? Your prompts and eye rolling took most of the fun out of our story. And I'm convinced that we didn't cover all of the details." Sulked a despondent Willing.

"So, what about the Selkie? What happened to her?" enquired an intrigued, Bub.

"Don't rightly know. We're thinking of heading back. First, we need to exact a bit of revenge on that so called 'King.' Honour my foot! He wouldn't recognise honour if it bit his bottom. Oh, that gives me such a delicious idea. You wanna come Bub? Not for the revenge part. We got that covered. Come meet the sad, but beautiful Selkie.

You'll need a full stomach. Can't travel on an empty stomach, now can you?

Oh, and just so you know, Willing. My bike is miles better than yours, so there." Fachance was pushing Harry out of the bed and miming fainting due to extreme hunger. Bub was wondering how they would explain the grocery budget deficit to Karen.

"Ah, hold that thought. We need to tell you about our latest adventure..." Harry added.

CHAPTER TWELVE

Devil Keith's room and he's a huffing...

"No, I categorically forbid it." Devil Keith was stamping the 6-inch stiletto heels on his sandal encased feet. He thought the new heels might need another 4 ounces of rainbow sequins to balance out the two, glued on flight-attendant Barbie dolls. He'd consult his sketches later then work out the Barbie to sparkle ratio. It was a complex theoretical physics formula that he planned on patenting then selling off to the highest bidder. However, he could only do this once he had expelled yet another brazen interloper from his private space.

"You have the best table, lots of comfortable chairs and a whiteboard. Plus, you still have half of Bub's old room. It has to be here. There's nowhere else." Pleaded Karen.

"No. No. No, you have a whole suite of offices. I think that you'll find that's 'somewhere else'. Definitely somewhere else, I'd say." Devil Keith awkwardly climbed over a camping stove, three red stripy deckchairs and then he viciously kicked a new Porta-loo. Discussion finished, as far as he was . He had a 1920's gold coloured flapper's dress that desperately needed some jet beads and fringing.

"But I don't want to share my offices. That's my sanctuary from all the madness in this joint. It's the only way I can function and deal with all your shenanigans." Moaned Karen as she sneakily slid a set of multi-coloured binders onto the dressmaking table. Only another ninety-six folders to go and she'd claim part of Devil Keith's office as her own.

"No, and that's final. Those Knights are already loitering in

my rooms and making them look really untidy. They're all chummy, chummy, and setting up tents with my best red, checked gingham fabric. My very best gingham!

Plus, I have to get away from them because if I hear another verse of Waltzing Matilda I may dance a blade right into one of their necks and/or stomachs. Repeatedly. Then there's some stupid, repetitive song about a smoking mountain and frenzied meatballs running down a hill. I'd run down a hill if a heard those yakking, yodellers coming anywhere near me. Plus, the song makes no sense... the meatballs would be disgusting and inedible once they had wandered around the undergrowth. The ninety-nine bottles of beer on the wall who, incidentally, keep going walkabout? Well, that's just asking to be chibbed on the chin with a broken bottle, and I'm the Devil to do it. Yes, I certainly am, missy.

No. This is my workspace. My place of inspiration. I enrich the world and besides, I don't have any fresh milk." Devil Keith finished his venting then stared at the contented Knights. *"Yes, I'm talking about you freeloaders. Sir Dan put that guitar back and step away from that bloody tambourine. No one is coming round any mountain while I'm here. And while we're at it. You lot get those camping stoves away from my silks. You fudging philistines. You're worse than that toad Harry."*

Karen knew when she was beaten so she agreed to use the conference rooms in her executive office, but she wasn't happy about it. Not happy, at all. The paperwork for Devil Keith's free vending machine access was about to disappear.

CHAPTER THIRTEEN

Karen's inner sanctum...

Harry was beside herself with glee. Not about the misplaced vending machine paperwork, duh. Devil Keith was on his own about that one. Although Harry would approve of Karen's deliberate admin mix up as she felt that she'd still not adequately punished Devil Keith for his many comments about her not being a real woman. And Devil Keith wouldn't stop sending Bub condolences cards and get well soon cards, as he believed that Bub was delirious and that was the only reason he had married Harry.

No, she was delighted by the room allocation argument. Good old stubborn Devil Keithie boy. He'd stuck to his guns. Harry had never seen the inside of Karen's offices and she hoped that it looked like a dominatrix's dungeon, or an olde sweetie shop, or a butterfly farm, or a prehistoric cave. She couldn't decide what she wanted it to be, and her suggestions were becoming increasingly odd. She probably needs to get herself a hobby or access to Netflix. Stat.

In retaliation for the whole room thing, Karen had borrowed the whiteboard and much to Devil Keith's horror she had wiped off all his Faery annihilation plans. However, he was confident that he and Brownie Anne could come up with an even more elaborate scheme to get those hovering baddies. Those Faeries had it coming. Uppity moths, the lot of them. Well the small ones were sorta moths, but the human sized ones all appeared to be remarkably successful business women.

The new monthly Hell staff meeting...

Karen shook out her bundle of papers and was now addressing the crowded room. *"Attention please. Only one biscuit per person and I hope you brought your own mug. Before you ask...I do not have herbal teas. I do not want herbal teas and no, I will not be getting any in the future. Right, settle down. We have a number of issues we need to work on. So, in no particular order.*

One. We have a dire shortage of space due to some, ahem, unforeseen circumstances. Bub, please get the walls and offices sorted out as soon as possible. That froufrou idiot just won't do it." Karen gave Devil Keith a hard stare, then snatched a second custard cream biscuit from his overstuffed mouth.

"I wouldn't exactly describe Harry as 'froufrou'. She's got more of a revolting, unwashed and undatable lumberjack vibe going on. Yes, definitely not froufrou." Devil Keith made a sad face at Harry, then cocked his head to the side, slowly blinked, and ever so tenderly patted his heart.

Harry playfully chucked an office chair at Devil Keith. Mr Hamhands so enjoyed his short flight, but the mid-flight safety brief left a lot to be desired as it only consisted of, *"oy, mind yerself"*. However the packet of complementary peanuts were delicious. He also enjoyed receiving the gift of a bright yellow plastic tabard with a whistle and a mini torch attached. He was going to keep that for his special date nights. Oh, sorry. Mr Hamhands was lounging on the thrown office chair. Just in case the authors weren't entirely clear.

"Two. We have a nemesis who is not only cruel, but he also lacks taste and fancies himself as some kind of theatre critic. He is currently languishing in and amongst an unusual trifle. I'm not exactly sure how we could have planned for that. Although, using the Interdimensional Drill to nip in and about other Hells without a formal invitation should have been a bit of a clue, ahem. Those high jinks resulted in us having to deal with extensive fire damage, blistering sunburn and an overspend on aftersun lotions." Karen

circled her notes with red ink.

"*All necessary. Eh, Bub, tell her?*" Devil Keith said, whilst spitting soggy crumbs all over Karen's carpet tiled floor.

"*Devil Keith, we need to use our inside voice just now. Yep, the one we keep inside our head.*" Whispered Bub as he dabbed at Devil Keith's crusty chin.

"*Three. We have minor demons from another Hell lodging with us, and we don't know if that's even allowed. Plus, we don't have any paperwork and no one appears to have a Job Description or a Job Plan. So who's paying their wages? Paying for their lodgings?*" Karen circled another item in red ink. The whole paper was beginning to look like an epic nosebleed.

"*Fudging parasites. The lot of them. Stop using my new knitting needles to spit-roast your dinner. Buy your own.*" Devil Keith growled and roughly pointed at the Knights. However, Mr Hamhands received a wee rub on his flat head and a long blow through his new shiny whistle.

"*Four. We are holding a dimensional object that belongs to another Hell. Again, are we even allowed to do that? Two seems greedy to me.*" Karen questioned and looked to the Knights for clarification.

"*Yep. I'm the Devil and that's just hunky-dory with me.*" Devil Keith nodded and shone the torch in his ear. He idly wondered how he could promote the ear canal as the next must have piercing spot.

"*That might need to go to a vote. Item five. There is the matter of the ravenous crocodile to contend with, and the subsequent repair bills. Ahem, talking of bills. I've seen the latest grocery bills. Can someone, maybe, try to speak with Fachance? Eh? Bags it's not me.*" Karen rapidly touched her nose with her index finger and was amazed that Devil Keith was nearly as fast as her. Bub had been taking some notes so he looked up to see the whole team touching their respective nose's and looking at him expectantly. And, it has to be said, the looks contained more than just a touch of pity. Oh no...

"On top of all that there are several observations from Gab, which need to be discussed and actioned. Apparently, the Oracles need an urgent review as their timelines are all in knots. He also slagged off our security measures and called them 'infantile.' Who knew there were so bad? Devil Keith please put your hand down. I'm convinced that you did not know that.

Plus, we still have some problems from book one that we haven't dealt with. So, I think we need to look at our policies, procedures, and punishments. That old Apple Mac computer is outdated, and I'm not convinced it's accurately reading the data any longer. The acid skin peels, the balaclavas and flesh-eating lady birds injected into the residents spinal column is so.... common and to be honest.... blah. It's all so passé.

So in conclusion. We need to liven it up and have some fun with our Hell. In a professional and solemn way, obviously. I can't stomach another lecture from the angelic Gab. So, my industrious and motivated team, give me a yeah." Karen waved her hands in the air and took a much-needed breath. She had decided that if she spoke at maximum speed and with as little detail as possible no one would realise just what a mammoth task they had to tackle.

Tumbleweed was the response.

"Karen, can you add Dippit and her repetitive fainting to the list?" Harry responded. She had been disappointed to find Karen's suite of offices were just humdrum, old 1960s or 1970s council offices. There were just various shades of brown, sludgy orange and beige walls with mismatched chairs and dying potted plants. A scarred Formica teak desk with broken locks on the drawers, and multiple coffee cup rings was abandoned in the middle of the room. Several large, lopsided, battered metal filing cabinets were haphazardly scattered around the exceedingly dull room. Harry had a quick peek in one of the drawers but even the stationery was standard issue. The drawers were stuffed with dog-eared, lined jotters and there wasn't so much as a lime

green highlighter in sight. The offices smelled like so many old offices do; of pencil shavings and the strange scent of old grey nylon tights left too long in a pair of scuffed, black, flat shoes.

There were no whips, or leashes, or giant gobstoppers, or heavily scented exotic flowers, or snoring, hibernating grizzly bears lurking about. What a lacklustre let down. There wasn't even a calendar, with a semi-clad fireman cuddling a fluffy wuffy kitten, on the squint notice board. Who can survive without the sight of a fireman, wearing only a Santa hat, stroking a contented puss?

Then Harry thought: there's probably a hidden room full of naughty and forbidden things. A secret room only accessible via a dastardly complex code, or via an impossibly complicated dance step, or via a dab of the correct flavour of ice-cream. Harry quickly discounted those ideas as she felt it was just a ludicrous, flight of fancy. A hobby it is then, and Harry decided to start collecting zombie garden gnomes. Well someone has to give the poor, misunderstood creatures a forever home.

"Dippit's fainting. Yes, we wanted to bring that up. That has to be the first order of business." Karen smiled at Dr Riel. He had made Karen breakfast in bed, and she had decided to talk Devil Keith into making her a new Evil, Wicked Stepmother outfit. She thought that Dr Riel deserved it, and their clandestine room needed to be christened. The discovery of the additional lust room was the only pleasant surprise following the whole Eva/ Karen episode.

After Karen had the space fumigated and some of the more exotic items were removed, she decided to keep the room *"just in case."* The maintenance men had liberated some of the rejected items and were currently using them as conversational door stops. Thankfully, the recreational items had visited a very, very blazing hot dishwasher setting before their new role. Karen was still struggling with the black leather adult swing, so she had filled the seat with trailing spider plants until she could work out how to use it without pulling the whole ceiling down. Dr Riel thought he might have found a solution to the ceiling problem so was popping over later with some Gorilla glue and a family sized pack of Dolly Mixtures.

CHAPTER FOURTEEN

Still in Karen's room…

A loud whoosh and a white tube fired across the conference room floor. Scattering the loose brown carpet tiles in its wake.

"What the…? Get down everyone." Bub dived for the tube and used his body to completely surround the foreign object. The teams screamed, scattered, and ran for cover. Bub waited a few seconds then gingerly rose to his feet. He looked at the tube, grabbed a chewed ruler and tentatively lifted the object from the floor.

"It's just a scroll. Thank goodness." Bub sighed and rubbed his sweaty palms on his trousers. But to be honest, so far nothing good had ever come from the receiving of a scroll but at least there were no Crabs or cigars attached to this one.

"How did it get here?" Harry could feel her anxiety levels increasing. Not more Hell number three problems? She was currently trying to toilet train a humungous crocodile and that was no easy task. The Angel Boy's babysitting favour was getting bigger by the second or to be more accurate: by the scented bucket load.

Bub peered down and pointed to a rotund mousehole in the skirting board. *"Well, we now know how Chick moved from place to place. I bet we'll all find mouseholes in our rooms. No wonder Hell number three had so much information about us."*

"What did my wee mate Chick do?" Devil Keith enquired and looked in the hole for his furry friend.

"Devil Keith, he was the secret Hell number three conspirator.

You unmasked him. A polar bear ate him. He's gone." Bub was shaking his head and pointing at Devil Keith's newly printed tee-shirt.

Devil Keith pulled at his tee-shirt, then cocked his head. He then did a quick handstand so that he could read the slogan. FYI, he still couldn't read it. *"The scruffy scoundrel. Wow, how clever am I? Did I do that recently?"*

"Yeah, I'll tell you all about it later." Bub sighed.

"Oh goodie. I like a good yarn." With that Devil Keith started on his next embroidery sampler titled *"chibbed in the chin for singing."* He was making a whole series for the loitering Knights and their newly created choir.

"Anyway, back to the scroll. Here's what it says:

'Yo, greetings, Hell number one.

Well done. You kick ass guys. We never thought you had it in you. You must really rock that one horn rating. We're well impressed." Bub read out loud. He was secretly very happy with the praise from the brutal pair.

"Not that I'm objecting, but Bub why do you sound like Liam Neeson?" queried Karen as she took a slug outta her mug of builder's tea.

"There's a button on the scroll that says hold for two seconds, so I did. It must change the reader's voice. Stan said that he was working on this, but I didn't know he had finished the project and had it out for use. Cool, eh? Right, can I continue with the scroll?

'So, dudes. We want to come to an arrangement. You give us more of those special cigars and some packs of cheesy balls. We take the Knights back and guarantee their safety. Sweet.

No problem if you can't get the cheesy balls: Aileen and Alanagh, the cooks, have been rattling up batches of cheese straws for us. We've confiscated Sir Muckle, Sir Fergus, and Sir Alan's water pistols...sorry boys. We converted them: they now fire garlic mayonnaise instead of swamp water. They're well sweet and compliment the cheese straws perfectly. We've permanently retired our Kalashnikov's for the mayo pistols; the shooting was giving us repetitive strain injuries anyway. Plus, all the screaming victims were affecting our hearing and we were at risk of being drummed out the highly coveted crustacean choir.

We've decided to stay on in Hell number three. It's laid back and we heard that the Knights want a say in running the place. We're cool with that. Less work for us. We just want the title of Devil, but none of the work. Sweet.

You can keep the cat. He's a beast and no one wants him back here. And we mean absolutely no one. We took a vote. He's dipped his last chocolate rat here.

Mr Hamhands can decide where he wants to live. Up to him. Odd wee guy, but sound as a pound. If he stays with you we can send his shoes on. Doubt you can get anyone else to make the strange, misshapen things and we've no use for them. They pinch our claws something fierce.

Old Roberto is welcome back, but we know he's still in a bit of a state so we can wait on his return. Angel Gab promised him some therapy, a long-term befriender, and a quick dip in a canal before he returns. That sounds pretty reasonable to us. Sweet.

The Dimensional Lance: that has to come back here so we're willing to negotiate. We only want to talk to Bub or Devil Keith about that. We won't talk to Karen, as she has a particular set of skills. She'd totally shaft us and we're not that brave. We need the Lance as soon as possible because we need to collect Melvin the Magician from Hell number eight and secure him in our dungeon. Seemingly his invisible doves are playing havoc with the grey squirrels and their hula-hoops. The mermaids are also complaining because he's a bit 'handsy'. We also need to hand in our notice to our old Hell. The Hell number eight twins might be laid back surfers, but they are sticklers for employment protocols.

Finally. We thought you might appreciate an update. King Adrian's still stuck in the jelly, and no one wants to go get him. We're not fussed. He's a bit of a tool so we're gonna leave him be. But if, or when, he gets out, he's getting plonked in with his lecherous brother. They can fight it out in one of the cells. You can come watch if you want. Should be a right rollicking laugh. Bring lots of cushions, the seats are hard on the old bahookee.

The Peacocks of Hell are off the hormone replacement therapy: at last. We couldn't take all the romantic movies and the tubs of Mackie's melted ice-cream. Plus, they had blocked the toilets with all their used tissues. Turns out that apart from Brian they're an ok bunch of birds. They're great at chess and a dab hand at the game Twister.

So, see ya Saturday, you crazy cats,
The Pincers aka the new Devils of Hell number three
Part-time drivers
Full-time lovers'
Well, that's a bit of a surprise. For a moment there I thought the scroll would be full of threats and at the very least, a declaration of war. Those cigars really did work a treat. We need to thank little Liam and Patrick for all their hard work. Talking of which; Karen, you did a bang-up job as the Evil Wicked Stepmother and Dr Riel, thanks for keeping everything running smoothly here. We couldn't have done this without you all," Bub had already thanked everyone else and was surprised at how much he enjoyed participating in the management duties. Maybe the angelic Gab had a point.

"That's a fudging relief. No offence Knights, but I'd rather feed you for a week than a fortnight. It's time for you to go back. If you can persuade Mr Hamhands to go with you then I can stop the pain of seeing his retreating denim clad bottom. I like you man, but denim? Really? Even the word makes me want to spew. Harry, you still need to burn my jeans and scatter the ashes on Kilimanjaro. Don't think I've forgotten that deal, you snotty 'Ginger Girl' layabout." Devil Keith snatched the biscuit tin from Harry's hands.

"Devil Keith, we have other things to worry about just now, but I'm sure ma wee darling Harry will get round to it. Lay off the 'Ginger Girl' comments if you know what's good for you." Bub stared at Devil Keith until Devil Keith gracelessly apologised to Harry.

"So, Saturday? As in tomorrow? Not much time to prepare," checked Karen. She was a bit miffed that she wasn't allowed

to negotiate as she most definitely did have a particular set of skills. She quite fancied the thought of a time share in a castle with unlimited access to all those manacles and pulleys.

"*Bub, sweetheart, pass me the scroll, please.*"

"*Devil Keith, you can have the scroll but stop calling me sweetheart. It's creepy,*" with that Bub threw the scroll at Devil Keith.

Devil Keith, Karen, and Harry began pressing the buttons and listening to the message again. Just to be clear: not to clarify the contents. Rather they found a rather irate Pingu version, an inebriated Popeye voiced version and a Chewbacca version of the message. They were wrestling the scroll from each other in order to look for other voices, and roaring with laughter at the results. That's until they found the Vin Diesel version. There was a decided hush as they listened: totally entranced by his dulcet tones.

"*Oh, Mr Moist Maker. His voice is so smooth it positively melts the elastic in my knickers.*" Devil Keith blushed.

"*I always thought you went commando. When did you start wearing knickers, Devil Keith?*" Harry was intrigued as she had seen his arse on many an occasion. Three thousand and fifty-two to be precise; she knew this as she had poked herself in the eyes each time. Totally worth the pain and tears, Harry thought.

"*Slipped on a silk pair a few seconds ago and they're just about to slide down to warm my ankles. Mmm, bliss.*" Devil Keith sighed and wriggled, ecstatically, in his chair.

"*Seriously folks. We need to make plans. Plus, be careful: according to Stan's project charter there's a Mr Bean button. I don't think that you want to have to mime the scroll. Dipping the rat in chocolate might be a bit of a tricky one.*" With that warning, Bub grabbed the scroll from the giggly group.

"*Bub, I'll go to Hell number three to negotiate. No need to interrupt your...yuck...honeymoon.*" Devil Keith bravely volunteered then gagged. And gagged some more.

"*Thank you, but sorry bro. I think I need to go. I'm not sure about handing over the Lance and whoever goes will have to carry the Drill so that they can get back out of that Hell. The Crabs could double cross us. They might end up with both of the devices and that would put us at a major disadvantage. Sorry, it needs some diplomacy. Actually, maybe a lot of diplomacy? Devil Keith, you have great style, but that level diplomacy might be a bit too much to hope for. You could always help with the Dippit situation? It's even more important and needs your subtle touch.*" Bub rubbed his brother's head.

Harry was shaking her head and drawing her index finger across her throat. She mouthed, "*Bub, Dippit will get you for this. No more dry-wipe markers for you.*"

"*Let's get started...*" with that announcement Karen started writing yet another "*to do*" list. In no particular order.

CHAPTER FIFTEEN

Bub and Harry's wrecked apartment...

"Oh, my goodness. What happened to you?" Harry hopped over a broken chair then rushed over to the injured Bub.

"I went to see a wee girly about a vicious cat." Bub was dabbing his torn lip and held a particularly bloody, slice of raw steak to his left eye.

"Oh, Periwinkle sure has a mean right paw. I meant to pack you some catnip, a cattle prod and a couple of juicy rats to distract him with." Harry had guided Bub to the sofa and was dabbing his lip. No kissing tonight. Prostitute sex it is then, she decided.

"This wasn't Periwinkle's doing. He was wrapped in a pink crocheted lace blanket and wearing a huge sunbonnet as he was wheeled about the glade in a bright yellow pram. He was in his element. He was purring and majestically waving at the Brownies. At one point I think he was shouting cooeey at me. To be honest, it kinda freaked me out. Did you know that his real name is John, but he preferred to be called Periwinkle? Changed it by Deed-poll. Odd, eh?

Turns out that Brownie Nelli has a bit of a protective streak when it comes to her 'kitty.' She got in a few decent hits before I could explain that it was Periwinkle's choice to go or stay. I wasn't there to steal him or force him back to Hell number three. No surprise: he's staying put. He is the most pampered cat I have ever had the misfortune to tangle with.

Brownie Hilary sends her regards. Well, more like bloody terrorisation and threats than regards. We are gonna have to find that wee dictator a fudging dog. And soon. She's stockpiling Brownie

Anne's bricks and I'm sure my name was written, in chalk, on a couple of them. Mac said that your name is now permanently scored into a few bricks, so we think that means that you really need to get your hands on a dog. And soon. She has a knife and appears to be willing to use it. I'll help because we aren't getting back there without one, and I kinda like discussing Phil Collins with Trevor. We've started our very own fan club." Bub was looking forward to designing some tasteful tee-shirts and other merchandise.

"It's on my 'to do' list. Karen has sunk a good bit of the budget into those yellow threats. As of this morning I have sixty-two of the Post-It 'requests' on my fridge. I'll work on them whilst you're gone. They'll help to keep me distracted and outta bother.

I'd really like to go with you, but I understand why we can't both go this time. Devil Keith has been hanging around Roberto and creating patterns for crocodile skin boots, belts, and handbags. He's already bought the tanning equipment and has it stashed under his bed. So, I need to keep your brother in check so that we can cash in the favour from Angel Boy.

I can't believe that G.O.D. still won't help us. I thought that after the Faery festival tickets and the proposal she'd forgiven us. Gab said she thinks we need to stop relying on her so much. I suppose that's true, but I really miss her and her thieving ways.

I have to admit that I'm not particularly bothered about keeping the crocodile safe: he's a fudging menace. He ate the base of our bed whilst you were with the Brownies. I'm pretty sure that those bed springs are gonna be tricky to digest and I have a real fear that he might need help ejecting them. I think I might have to help unwind them out of his bottom, again. I've been throwing tubs of Vaseline, bottles of castor oil and huge chunks of lard at him. Just in case I have to 'Colon Corkscrew' him again. That's what I'm calling it now. I can't believe I have a name for that procedure.

I already had to unwind the shorter, sofa springs out of him. The thought of doing it again, with the longer bed springs, makes me boak. Dave, the kennel master, already said he won't help. He said that the Hounds of Hell keep him busy all of the time. I'm not entirely sure if that's true. I saw holiday brochures for Disney World and Disney Land, open on his desk. I think he has a thing for Minnie Mouse. I pity that poor rodent. I really do." Harry finished her rant with a shudder.

"Why were you checking under Devil Keith's bed? No never mind. I'm glad you did it, saves me the bother. Hopefully, the bed springs will make an appearance before I leave. We can bond over the vomitous task. Talking of leaving. Is everything set?" the bleeding had stopped but the black eye was gonna be a doozy. Bub was now no longer convinced that he enjoyed management duties... or Brownies.

CHAPTER SIXTEEN

Bub and Harry's crowded, wrecked apartment…

All of the Hell number three Knights and Mr Hamhands were leaving with Bub. They missed their own home and wanted to make some positive changes to Hell number three. The Knights were planning a democracy, and as such, the elections were happening as soon as they got home. Devil Keith had insisted on helping with the campaign slogans and posters. As a result, the posters were all very confusing with slogans such as, *"lucky old you, you'll think you're in Hell number one,"* or *"you know how to do, so just do it"* and lastly, *"we will make the King wear underpants."*

Harry thought that there may not be too many folks casting their votes or even understanding how to vote. Devil Keith was also insisting that all voters had to wear a very specifically themed tiara. That was also causing some issues as the tiaras had to contain a painted Easter egg worthy of Fabergé himself and have five rabbit's feet trailing from the back. The rabbit feet were to be DNA checked to ensure that they were all from the same rabbit. No, not too many five-legged rabbits out there. So, not too many voters predicted Harry. She knew those posters were heading straight for the bin, although she'd pay good money to see those tiaras and meet those rabbits.

The triplets were taking some cockroaches with them when they leave. They were totally fed up with their tricycle and its inability to traverse the castle's many sets of steep stairs. They felt that they were spending far too much time in the local accident and emergency department. It was negatively impacting on their ability to creatively gamble. Afterall, there's a limit on the number of times you can, *"guess the number of stitches that fit on a big toe'"* or *"guess the number of enemas required to remove a bike spoke."*

The triplets were also fed up with wearing their restrictive cycling helmets. Sir Fergus had taken quite a shine to the be-ribboned bonnets that were covering his bald pate and so wanted them included in his summer wardrobe. Sir Alan thought the helmets covered up too much of his glorious blonde mane so were putting off the ladies. What ladies?

Lastly, Sir Muckle was still having some issues with keeping his head at right angles to his shoulders. The wing mirrors were painfully digging into his left shoulder, poor wee soul. He had decided that he needed to get home to get some of his special glue. The glue had previously repaired his IKEA bookshelves so it would probably restore his crushed vertebrae. He decided that a good, big dollop of glue and some Popsicle sticks would make a fine neck brace. A fine brace indeed.

The triplets had decided that they were going to breed the Hell cockroaches and make a fully automated walking pavement. As they had never been allowed a pet before they wanted to name the cockroaches. So there were likely to be as many disagreements and injuries over that as they usually had with their troublesome tricycle. There are only so many cockroaches that could answer to the name Mary, without total carnage ensuing.

Roberto the crocodile was staying in Hell number one as he didn't feel up to seeing the castle moat yet. It was triggering him. Gab was planning on a course of Cognitive Behavioural Therapy and Mindfulness for the handsome crocodile. Harry was still, very much, crocodile sitting and hating every spring coiled moment of it.

Cute Mr Hamhands wanted to start his own line of vending

machines. He was rather taken with the pilchard tea, whale blubber coffee and the range of squid tacos in the Hell number one machines. Also, due to his uncontrollable fist bumps he was on the maintenance crews *"Most Wanted"* list. The crews were fed up with patching up the holes in the walls and then re-plastering them. It was proving to be a nightmare to re-nicotine stain the surfaces so as to match up the older colours and patches. Plus, digging people out of the holes in the walls was initially fun but now they just couldn't spare the manpower. Karen had the crew working through some very long lists. She had snuck a secret room ceiling repair onto the list as the Dolly Mixture's paste hadn't fixed the problem with the adult swing.

Although still fragile, Willing had insisted on accompanying Bub on his mission. For her peace of mind, she wanted to make sure that the King was still ensconced in the strawberry jelly and covered with killer rubber ducks. Dr Riel agreed that it would help with her mental health and recovery. She was also intrigued by the Crabs and wanted to ask them what they knew about Selkies and their wayward skins.

Fachance decided to stay in Hell number one. She was still growing back her thumbs so she wanted the additional time to heal. She was also enjoying the kitchen privileges, although she thought the store cupboards were a little bit bare and needed a good *"sort."* Bub feared that sort was another name for *"eat on an empty stomach"* or just her usual insatiable hunger. He remained very much gobsmacked at the amount the dainty glutton could pack away.

CHAPTER SEVENTEEN

Bub and Harry's apartment and departure minus ten minutes...

"Everyone have everything they need? Sir Mark, do you really need that second side of bacon? If you put it back then I'm sure that Fachance would stop slapping you about the head and kicking your shins." Bub queried and narrowly missed a kick himself.

Sir Mark began laughing at that preposterous idea. He would always need that second side of salty goodness. The team looked at each other and rammed their fingers in their ears as the laugh grew louder and louder. They risked being drawn into his fatal fun.

A small, malevolent creature slithered across the floor towards the frivolity. The misshapen crawler was on a mission to wipe Hell number one from existence. It had dug, clawed, and sliced its way out of a dark and hideous chasm. It had committed acts that would sicken the most stalwart of evil beings. It was hell bent on exacting vengeance on the populous.

It skulked closer to the laughing Knight. Unable to stop its curiosity and blood lust. It coughed, then laughed, then giggled, then laughed some more and felt something important break loose in its revenge filled body. As its lungs and left heart ventricle sailed out of its nostrils it screamed. *"I fudging hacked my way out of that polar bear's intestines, using only a darning needle and a thimble with an enamel picture of Glasgow's George Square on it, only to die like this?"*

There was a splat. The team were oblivious to the little

THE DEVIL'S A HUNTING

angry mouse and his offal (awful) death.

"Sir Andrew, can you put Mr Hamhand's business plan in your rucksack? I have a spare tool kit, for him, that might just come in useful. Do you have space for that too?" Bub handed over the package.

Mr Hamhands began doing star jumps and pointing in the air. Bub looked at Harry in confusion. What could have gotten the happy chap in such a tizz?

"I've got this." Devil Keith crossed his legs, put his elbow on his knee and rested his chin on his knuckle. *"Please continue and I will pass on your wishes to these mere minions."* Devil Keith sagely nodded whilst sneaking in a kebab drenched in extra chilli sauce and topped with a crumble of bourbon creams. Afterall, the wee guy deserved a nice treat in his cheek pouches.

Mr Hamhands mimed fighting a huge, black, gluttonous wolverine. The hungry skunk-like creature that had caught Mr Hamhands' head in his mammoth jaws and was dragging him away for dinner. During dinner Mr Hamhands appeared to convince the skunk that becoming a vegetarian was a positive life choice. The skunk cried, then gave Mr Hamhands a complex and colourful goodbye wave.

"Really? Interesting. Please continue." Devil Keith slowly nodded and placed a monocle in his left eye.

Mr Hamhands then began using an office chair to mime swimming across a lake and cradling partially sighted turtles to his breast. Turtles who then turned on him and were massaging him to death. Mr Hamhands appeared to fight them off with lavender scented hand lotion and a body scrub. He escaped unscathed.

"You never did, and that's what happened? Terrible." pondered Devil Keith, whilst shaking his head then wiping his hands on the back of Harry's shirt.

Mr Hamhands then mimed being caught in quicksand and fighting off marauding mosquitoes. Eventually capturing the butch biters in a fragile butterfly net and releasing them back into the wild. Ensuring they were first appropriately spayed and neutered.

"*Quite right too. Can't fault you on that one.*" Devil Keith dusted off his hands and blew his nose on Harry's sleeve.

Mr Hamhands stopped. Then bowed. There was complete silence then a rousing round of applause complete with cries of "*Bravo*" and "*Bravissimo*".

Harry wiped away a small tear and picked up the flowers that had been thrown at Mr Hamhands' feet. She then asked Devil Keith if she had correctly understood the wee guy's acting skills and sign language. Harry was still learning sign language as she didn't want to be as ill prepared as the bombastic King.

Devil Keith slowly shook his head, then said. "*Nope, you bizarre brain-dead female. He clearly needs some of your Egyptian knick-knacks so he can nail a woman he saw in the castle kitchens. Her name's Judy and she has tattoos of the pharaohs on her arms, so Mr H thought he'd have a go when he got back. He wants to raise his own footstools. I think they were footstools or maybe just some stools.*"

"*Mr Hamhands, is Devil Keith correct? All that so you can get a wife?*" Harry was aghast.

Mr Hamhands began enthusiastically nodding at Devil Keith. He began pointing at Harry's shelves. Harry shrugged then passed him a miniature pyramid, a bauble and a vial of gnats milk. Mr Hamhands started another joyous round of star jumps. Harry decided that she urgently needed more lessons in sign language...and understanding men.

Still preparing to leave...

"*Sir Fergus of D'Fries, please don't panic, Devil Keith added a few spare sets of ribbons and some daisies for your hats. Sir Muckle, that neck brace needs to come off in the next couple of hours. Dr Riel said to remind you that it was only a temporary measure to get you safely home. Your new design and special glue sounds much more robust and satisfying.*

Sir Andrew, your vegan monthly subscription's been re-directed to Hell number three. If it arrives here, we'll forward it on to you.

Sir Spark, thank you for helping to re-wire the offices and especially for fixing up my oven. The wiring has never been the same since the incident with the Occulites." Harry shook Sir Spark's smoky hand.

Stan had previously rigged Harry's cooker to sing *"Hot stuff,"* by the very talented Donna Summer, when the oven had reached the perfect temperature for cooking her chicken and pineapple pizza. Since the Occulites fire, steam, and water damage it had taken to singing *"Everybody Hurts"* by REM. Stan hadn't had the time to make the necessary repairs so it was great having Sir Spark's to re-wire and get the gifted Ms Summer back on track.

"Harry, my darling wifey, a kiss before I go?" smiled and winked Bub. He opened his arms wide.

"Oh well. If I must." Harry leapt into Bub's arms and smothered his face in tiny kisses.

"Gonna be sick. Yuck, yuck, yuckety, yuck." Devil Keith gagged into a pillow.

"Devil Keith, gives a hug, ya big lug."

"Oh well. If I must." Devil Keith jumped across the sofa and grabbed Bub in a tight bear hug.

"One last thing. Before you go. Sir Derek. Going by the size of your big hands I think it's fair to say that you could hold your laptop open at a game of Freecell and still manage to carry a sword." Harry grinned over Bub's shoulder then passed Sir Derek a small butter knife.

"Classy bird. We'll miss you all. Don't be strangers." Laughed Sir Derek as he moved a Queen of Hearts onto the King.

Willing hugged Harry and kissed Devil Keith on the forehead. Bub put the Drill against the wall, and they left via the glowing portal.

P AND K STOKER

CHAPTER EIGHTEEN

Bub and Harry's apartment...

The portal had barely faded when Stan charged through from Karen's office into Harry's domain. Karen thought that it was just like Piccadilly station in her executive suite. Everyone seemed to think that they could just barge in then use it as a corridor to where they really wanted to be. Twice now, she had found Harry tapping and listening at the walls. She was convinced that Harry was looking for her secret room. The nosey wee Harpy.

Stan was carrying a bright green and unconscious Dippit. *"Dr Riel. Your help. Your help, now. Please."*

Dr Riel rushed over and began checking Dippit's vitals. *"She's fainted but it appears much deeper than before. Have you tried to rouse her?"*

"She's been like this for forty minutes and yes, I fudging well have tried to rouse her. Sorry, I'm at my wits end. I'm so worried. This is getting worse. Dippit can barely manage to eat or drink without collapsing. Yesterday, she nearly drowned in the bathtub. I told her I would help her, but she said that I needed to stop fussing over her. How can I stop fussing over her? I love her and our baby." Stan was clearly distressed as the repetition had stopped and panic had well and truly started.

"Stan, Stan. I need you to concentrate. Take a deep breath. We've got her. I just need some more information. I need you to think. Did your mum have this severity of symptoms?" Dr Riel was proving to be a real G.O.D. send. They had decided not to say

God as they couldn't take the disappointment when she didn't immediately appear brandishing her hostess trolley and her lucky rabbit's foot lighter.

"No, my mam's symptoms were pretty mild compared to what my Dippit is going through. Mam turned the colour of blanched celery and had a few dizzy spells each day, but she quickly recovered. The only other odd thing was my mam's craving for fresh grass. The green stuff cow's eat, not the other kind. She's as puzzled as I am. My mam's trying to hide it, but she's as worried as I am. Mam's convinced that Dippit is losing weight and her hair is getting pretty brittle and falling out. She's lost all her gorgeous curls. Dippit's also becoming grossly dehydrated. Her skin is paper thin and dry. We're all at our wits end. Even Liam and Patrick are completely stumped by this development. That probably worries me more than anything else." Stan was visibly trembling and gently stroking Dippit's thinning, flat hair. There was evidence of recent tears on his quivering cheeks.

"I'm sad to say this, but your mum's right. We're going to have to put Dippit on bed rest and get some fluids into her. Bring her with me, please." Dr Riel left with the distraught father to be.

"Karen, we have to do something. I'm so worried about her. I think we need to call on Gab and see if he can help us. Gab!" Harry screamed at the ceiling.

Karen heard the adult swing fall from the ceiling again and hoped that Harry hadn't twigged on what the noise was.

CHAPTER NINETEEN

Bub and Harry's apartment...

"*Angel Gab, time to call in that favour. Please.*" Harry solemnly requested.

"*Already? I thought you would make me sweat for a week or two, Ginger Girl.*" Said the perfectly attired Angel.

"*Don't think that hasn't crossed my mind, but enough of the old flirting... Angel Boy. Make you sweat? In your dreams.*

We need your help. Dippit's having a terrible time of it. She keeps flushing dark green and fainting. She barely has time to eat and drink between bouts. It's causing us all to worry. Stan's beside himself with worry and he's stopped repeating himself." Harry attempted a smile and a bit of sarcasm, but her heart just wasn't in it.

"*Flirting? What flirting? I would never ever, ever flirt with you. That is your gross misconception. Oh, even the thought is nauseating. Bub is such a brave man to take you on.*

So, what do you need? I mean in relation to Dippit. Again, I would never, ever flirt with you, Ginger Girl. Oh, wait. Stan is not repeating himself? Really?" Gab was uneasy with the tone of the conversation and starting to waffle. He was also backing away from Harry in case she made a move on him. This whole conversation was terribly confusing as Gab was always prepared for the worst when Harry called on him.

Harry put him out of his misery. No, she didn't shoot him. Although to be fair, she could, and would if he didn't help her. She smiled as she thought about feeding the oversized budgie some out of date bird seed then hiding the loo roll.

"*I need you to cure our Dippit and stop the rate of deterioration she's facing. Make her well again. Please.*" Harry pleaded and her voice broke at the end.

"*I am sorry Harry. Dippit is not unwell, per say. She is pregnant. I cannot cure that.*" Gab was glad that Karen was chaperoning the bizarrely polite conversation.

"*Angel Gab. You take everything so fudging literally. I mean, can you stop the flushing and fainting? Please. I'm saying please and being genuine. That would wipe your slate clean.*" Harry pleaded again.

"*I am naturally suspicious of you and all you do, so please forgive me for taking time to process your request.*

Right... I do not think I can do anything. I do not know what you and your sisters are, so I would surmise that the issue is with your genetic makeup and how Dippit's has combined with Stan's. I heard his origin story and although rare, it has happened before but only once that I know of. I have also previously heard about the green flushing, dizzy spells, and occasional fainting but nothing on the scale that you are describing." Angel Gab was pacing around the room and scratching his head. This was a puzzle.

"*Ah, I see what you mean. So how do we work out what's wrong? How to fix this?*" Harry stared at the bemused Angel.

"*I would suggest that you consult the Oracles. They may be able to tell you about Dippit's past and whether that is the reason for the severity of the pregnancy side effects.*" Gab nodded as he offered the possible solution.

"*Please, not the Oracles. Can't you just flash us back in time to Dippit's mam, or to our father so we can ask one of them?*" Harry hopefully stated.

"*Sorry, my flashing, as you so quaintly put it, has set rules. As you are aware I can only flash a limited number of times within a specified time frame. I cannot move through time. That is an altogether different skill set that I do not possess.*

What about the Time Viewer? That would allow you to observe the past but not alter it. It is safe and even you could not make a mistake when using it." Gab helpfully suggested.

"Ah well, about that." Wriggled Harry as she sheepishly looked down at the floor.

"Yes, Harry?" Angel Gab was stretching his wings ready to leave.

"Bub broke it." Harry whispered.

"HE WHAT? That is a special artefact. It is irreplaceable. It is designed to let an individual view a story and gain truths about their lives. Please tell me that you are joking. Even your team could not be that clumsy. That irresponsible. I think I may need to go lie down in a darkened room." Gab started wafting his wings, as he too had taken on a greenish tinge. He really could do with a Falkirk Sewer or a long vacation. Maybe just some ear plugs so he could ignore the Ginger Banshee.

"Eh, no. I'm not joking. It's gone. Snapped in half. I tried to glue it back together again, but it kept taking me to view the 1966 World Cup final. I'm Scottish and I hate football so, in truth, it was all a bit of a nightmare. Then it took me to some nauseating Dressage Events. Oh, they are so sick and twisted. And for the last few viewings I've gone to a walking stick museum. The museum wasn't too bad, especially when you consider the quality of the other jaunts." Harry said all of that as if it was a reasonable conversation to have with the unsteady Angel.

"This is bad. So Bad. The Oracles already have a poor track record, and this might push them over the edge. Erm, let me think...I need a minute.

Well, there is nothing else for it, Ginger Girl. The Oracles it is then, and I really hope they are in a good mood today." Gab was pacing around and plaiting his long, glossy hair. He was also systematically pulling out his fringe and flinging the hair behind him.

Harry knew this was a big ask. *"Well in that case. That's my favour. You deal with the Oracles, get the answer from them, and then fix Dippit."*

"Mmmm. That would be ideal and remove the promise you

have over me, but alas I cannot do this on my own as I am not convinced that your Oracles are working properly. I did say that you needed to address that but as you have not done so I fear that this may be too complex for one individual to handle." And Gab had so hoped that he could get out from under that oath he made to Harry.

"Ok but you need to come with me so that I know what I'm looking for." Harry bargained.

"That I can do. After all the Oracles make a mouth-watering bread and butter pudding. I am sure Roberto would love a little treat after suffering the indignities of the bed springs removal. Harry, did you and Bub have to use such a large, industrial magnet? I am sure that castor oil alone would have done the trick." Gab tutted and shook his head in disappointment.

"Angel Boy, there isn't enough castor oil in the whole wide world to deal with that crocodile's intestines. Trust me! We checked! Repeatedly! So, off we go." Harry clarified and pointed at the door.

CHAPTER TWENTY

The Oracles abode…

Gilbert and Marjorie were having a wee break from their Oracling. Is that even a thing or a word? The authors must think that they're Shakespeare and are now just making up words and hoping they then get added to the dictionary. The fudging cheek of them.

Anyway, the Oracles were lounging on their sofa and contemplating their next super purchase. What they really should have been doing is:

Finding their lost Big Bang Runes: the most important chunks of rock in all of history. The Runes predicted the future, and they kept the Oracles focused on the present timeline. The Oracles internal time clock was out of whack and the pizza box with the Ryan Reynolds' (R.R.) tomato stain wasn't as accurate as they required. In fact, they had gotten a wee smidgen drunk, on cherry brandy, and then ordered more pizzas. As a consequence of being rather squiffy, they now had eleven pizza boxes. All with possible RR sightings and stains. This had gotten so out of hand that Marjorie had stuffed the empty-ish boxes under their burgeoning sofa. Denial is a wonderful thing.

The Oracles should also be selling some of their previous purchases as they were at risk of drowning in empty Nile boxes and un-popped bubble wrap. Their hoarding had taken on truly gargantuan proportions, and they also risked the local loan sharks' battering down their door for payment. The ever increasing, red credit card bills were sitting right next to the stained pizza boxes. Consequently, the legs on the sofa now hovered above the floor and Gilbert needed a small set of steps to climb onto said sofa. Marjorie used her school days pole vaulting skills to ascend the foamy, floral mound.

Cataloguing their dangerous artefacts should also figure on their to-do list. They had completed their mandatory, theory security training but the practical was proving tricky to enforce. Alas, there was an Australian soap opera on their 280-inch flat screen TV and it was holding their rapt attention. They had made the executive decision that security breaches were as rare as hen's teeth so they would just top up their Aussie accents instead. After all, how bad could things get? They should know, and boy they didn't understand the irony.

Plus, they really should be re-stocking their jukebox as they had been playing the same set of records since 1962. Earlier that day Gilbert had put his back out again whilst doing the Hucklebuck. Plus, Marjorie was fed up with all the walking up and down his crooked spine. Gilbert wasn't so keen on that either as his Marjorie was no dainty pixie. Gilbert could attest to that fact as he had surreptitiously checked out Paula the Pixie's statistics and Marjorie didn't make the grade, even on her *"no scrumptious baked camels day"*.

Gab and Harry need a favour...

The Oracles were delighted to welcome Gab and Harry to their cluttered home. There was no clean crockery available so the visitors were served Ribena blackcurrant juice in a set of cracked, leaking egg cups. Whilst their slices of cake went straight from the hot oven tray into their fluffy pockets. Gab was a wee tad disappointed as the Oracles Empire Biscuits were usually quite delicious, plus the scalding cake had melted his emergency pack of plastic hair clips. He needed to keep the hair clips to hand in case he failed to attend his daily haircut. His long hair was glorious and turned many a head. The regular haircuts ensured that he didn't turn into a vacuous Rapunzel and be harassed by the local builders. And short sighted, randy Princes. They too posed a constant risk to his luscious, dark locks.

Gab and Harry quickly brought the Oracles up to date. Marjorie and Gilbert were delighted with Dippit and Stan's news, although they were all concerned about Dippit's pregnancy developments.

"Oh, a wee baby, we haven't seen one of them for such a long time. Has it been a long time, Marjorie? I can never quite work that out. Oh, just think… a squishy, pink baby to squeeze and spoil and bake for.

Tell Dippit that we really must insist on babysitting. Oh, and we have twenty or thirty prams she can have. We'd have to sell them at cost or just a shade above cost. Things are a bit tight just now… money wise." Gilbert was giddy with delight at the prospect of a baby cuddle and paying off some of the loan sharks. He did so enjoy having his own kneecaps hanging around his person.

"Thanks…I'll pass that on. What we really need is a cure for Dippit's flushing and fainting. She's really unwell and getting worse. We think she's only a day away from being completely bald and totally unrousable." They're also getting worse thought, Harry. Angel Boy was correct; the insufferable know it all.

"Mmmm. Yes, I can see why you're so worried. We don't have a cure for that. We don't really know what you Horsewomen are. Have you tried asking your father? He might still be around and about." Marjorie suggested as she offered them a bin bag full of start shaped sugar cubes.

"Stan's already tried that, but he can't find Roger. Stan's normally really lucky so if anyone was going to stumble on the serial adulterer's lair it would be him." Harry wasn't bitter at all. No, not at all.

"Erm, unfortunate. Let me think. Well in that case you could ask Dr Riel to borrow the Time Viewer. I'm sure he should still have it to hand. You could use that to see if your mothers had the same

problems. What they did about it. That would help. In fact, I'd go so far as say that would solve this problem." Marjorie brushed her hands together. She was delighted that she could help. She thought that they might not have helped for quite some time, but she wasn't sure what that time could be. It was all a bit confusing.

"*Ah. About that. Hmmm. The Time Viewer is... broken?*" mumbled, Harry.

"*WHAT the fudge!!*" Gilbert screamed and took back the bag of sugar lumps.

CHAPTER
TWENTY-ONE

D evil Keith's office and design studio…

"*Stan, I'm glad that Dr Riel allowed you and Dippit out of the health centre. Is she any better?*" Harry patted Stan's freezing cold hands.

"*Not really. I say, not really but I thought I'd be more useful here. I say, more useful here. Plus, I'm not so keen on Jonathan being near my Dippit. He's saying some really horrible things about her hair. How Dippit looks a dead ringer for Gollum from Lord of the Rings. Lord of the Rings, I say. I don't think Jonathan's a nice person. I say, not nice at all and I thought we were friends. Friends, I say.*" Stan was both sad and angry at that development.

"*Karen and I will deal with that rotter Jonathan later. He won't be saying much after that. Lord of the Rings? I'll give him …*

Anyway, I'm glad you're all here it saves me repeating this later. Well, the good news is that we got the Time Scavenger from the Oracles. That will help us find Roger. The Oracles are not happy as that really cuts into their time jumping shopping expeditions. The bad news is that we are going to have to find the Big Bang Runes for the Oracles. Oh, that's why our Oracles have been having such an issue with keeping track of time. They misplaced their sacred Runes.

Marjorie and Gilbert said that finding the fudging Runes would be a dangerous mission, but they wouldn't budge on that deal. We have to do this for them, or else. They were furious about the broken Time Viewer. I'm surprised you didn't hear them shouting;

the walls were violently shaking, and we were temporarily caught in an avalanche of Nile boxes. I never realised, but Marjorie has a truly brutal imagination. I think she might be able to help us develop more creative punishments for Hell number one. Although I'm pretty sure some of her suggestions were anatomically impossible and a bit on the nippy side. Luckily, we persuaded the Oracles to let us use the Time Scavenger to help Dippit before having to find their Runes.

So, there are quite a lot of risks and rules when using the Time Scavenger and we promised to tell you all about them. Just in case something goes horribly wrong, and you have to mount a rescue operation. If it comes to it, please, please rescue us. I don't want to be trapped in a time that had no curry flavoured Pot Noodles, train timetables, or the fudging Kardashians to laugh at. The Bronte sisters brushed over all those inconveniences in their books, but it was grisly stuff back then.

Plus, if we damage the Time Scavenger Marjorie promised that she will wear my skin as an overcoat. I thought she'd only have enough skin for a scarf, but she was adamant that it would stretch to a long coat, a hat, AND a scarf. Bit cruel I thought. So please don't mess any of this up. Pretty please." Harry was visibly shaken and longed for Bub's cool head for business. Even a cuddle would help. Really help about now. Where was a rescuing Adonis when you needed one? Oh right, Hell number three, duh.

The rules...

Harry explained that unlike the Time Viewer, which allowed you to view but not interact with a scenario, the Time Scavenger was fully interactive. That could be dangerous as it had the potential to change history. So they needed a small, responsible team who knew the detailed history of the time period they were visiting. That way they would be less likely to accidentally change something in the past that would rebound on the now. The Oracles strongly recommended that Devil Keith was left in Hell number one. Just as a precaution. The Oracles hadn't forgotten how difficult it was to keep Devil Keith away from making a sandwich with the Evil French Loaf. The fact that the Oracles could accurately remember the details of that interaction demonstrated, to Harry, just how important the advice about Devil Keith really was.

The Oracles also suggested that a member of the time team should regularly check back with present day Hell so that they could be confident that nothing historical relevant had been changed. The present-day team would only know the new history of the period so the time traveller could compare notes. That would allow the time travelling team to rectify mistakes and put history back on track. That was the hope anyway.

Time travel was mighty tricky, and ideally they would have asked G.O.D. for access to Einstein but she was still a bit miffed with the Hell team. Einstein was also still recovering from C.C.'s multiple time realignments (the authors suggest that you see book one for details and assure you that they are not just making the suggestion to boost sales, but that would be nice).

"So, in summary. We need a top-notch researcher who can catalogue the Renaissance period and provide a potted history that Angel Boy and I can easily memorise. Oh, Gab I meant to tell you this before, when we were with the Oracles. Unfortunately you were looking so harassed by all the staples and packing peanuts caught in your lengthy locks that Gilbert and I didn't want to disturb you. We went through our options, but it would be good to double check the plan, in case we missed something important." Harry added.

"Good idea. Those packing peanuts are sentient beings and as such I had to talk them out of my tangled hair. They had a mighty persuasive argument to stay put, but I won them over. I now have a regular crazy golf game to add to my calendar. But please continue." Gab said all of this without cracking a smile. Harry could never fathom how that partial penguin-type being ticked. Harry always thought of Gab as a penguin because she thought he was so stiff and uptight all of the time. And he could be doing with being pushed off an ice shelf into the jaws of an orca.

How they chose the correct time period...

Harry presented their reasoning. *"Okkkkay. So, we had hoped to visit Dippit's time as that would be the most relevant and most likely to answer all our questions regarding her condition. Unfortunately, due to the changes in calendars it's so hard to define the exact date we need. The ancient Greeks were surprisingly gifted at astrology and astronomy but just not quite good enough to pin down an exact enough time. Plus, there are too many Greek islands to visit and thoroughly search. So finding a precise location was also going to be problematic. Added to those issues is the fact that the Greek people were forever philosophising and searching for themselves. We could easily miss Helena and Roger as they gazed longingly at their navels'. So, all in all, it was not a promising hunting option.*

We discussed visiting my time period but there were some unsurmountable problems. It's a shame really because as a Druid Priestess my mam would have been such an asset to our current issue. Unfortunately we can't visit my village as Bub completely destroyed all evidence of its existence. If we were lucky enough to find it, then it's so small that we wouldn't be able to hide our presence. Village people can get a wee touch tetchy and strangers, at that time, would make them a big touch tetchy. Plus, we are at a much higher risk of changing things as there is so little known about that time period. So, as you can see that was a non-starter.

Although, I would still really love to see my mam again. She was such a beautiful person, inside and out. Maybe if we can keep the Time Scavenger for a little bit longer that would be possible. After we find the Runes and save my epidermis, that is.

We could visit Willing's time as that's well documented and likely to be the most accurate time frame but unfortunately we can't because..."

Harry explained that Willing was born in late 1915 to a buoyant and enthusiastic young woman called Maisie, and a seemingly contented Roger. Maisie had wanted to be an actress from when she was a small child and saw her first risqué vaudeville production. She'd sit in the darkened theatre and be whisked off to another life. A life of drama, humour and intrigue. She'd close her eyes in fear when she thought the limber acrobats would fall off the stage, she'd giggle at the comedians comic faces and she'd raucously sing along with the bawdy songs. Then ask her embarrassed mother what the words meant. However, it was the actors and actresses who claimed her heart.

As Maisie got older she decided that she wanted to be a silent movie actress as she absolutely adored the actress, Mary Pickford. You'd often find young Maisie draped in lace curtains and dramatically whispering the lines, from the very latest hit, to her extremely patient cat. She devised her own deportment lessons and would sweep her mother's kitchen floors whilst balancing a book on her head. A book that frequently fell off, and resulted in her cat having a very flat tail and reluctantly moving in with the elderly next door neighbours. Maisie also collected cinema posters, stood at stage doors on cold winter nights to grab an elusive autograph and she obsessively clipped out reviews from all the local newspapers.

Just before falling for the dashing Roger, Maisie had managed to land herself a job in a local theatre. She was a hard-worker and the manager told her that she was an up and coming showgirl with considerable talent, legs to her chin and a cheeky infectious grin. He was smitten with the gorgeous Maisie. As it happens, Roger saw Maisie on stage one night and he was entranced by her beauty, laughter and joie de vivre. He had to have her. He waited at the drafty stage door with a box of Belgian chocolates, a posy of hothouse flowers and a mouthful of boundless flattery. Roger promised Maisie fame, fortune and a place on the silver screen. He gave Maisie a child.

Roger was occasionally a reasonably successful travelling salesman who used his considerable charm to sell buttons and general haberdashery items, at that time. He used the extensive railway networks to travel all over the country and consequently he was rarely at home most weeks. Little Willing use to describe her joy when she'd see her father's old battered, brown leather suitcase propped up in the hallway of their tenement apartment. That meant he was home so she'd have long cuddles, bags of sweeties, receive odd gifts and experience wonderful stories that night. Depending on how well Roger's travels and sales had gone, Willing would receive a stolen crystal sherry glass from the first class buffet car or an old cork from the floor of a freight car. However, Roger being home also meant that Maisie would take a precious night off to stay with her daughter and husband. Willing didn't care what gift she received as she kept them all in a series of precious cigar boxes hidden under her bed.

Roger kept to that lifestyle until Willing was around seventeen years old and then he joined a local bootlegging gang. He was based in Chicago but continued to enjoy a nomadic lifestyle, albeit with a lot more ready cash. Little did Maisie know but Roger's change of profession had little to do with her dissatisfaction at being left alone so often and her need for money for urgent medical care. His change of career had more to do with his need to save money so he could high tail it outta there.

Purely coincidentally, Harry and Devil Keith had visited Chicago around the same time that Roger must have still been there in the bootlegging business. In theory that should make things so much simpler as they had local knowledge and contacts. Plus, access to a network of hoodlums and lunatics (the bootleg gin wasn't so good for the old noggin). As an added bonus, it was a big city so they could easily sneak in and out without being noticed. The snag was that Devil Keith and Harry had been partying pretty hard during their time in Chicago.

CHAPTER TWENTY-TWO

Back in the day, in old Chicago town...

Devil Keith and Harry were at a local Speakeasy, listening to some excellent early blues music, when things went a little bit pear-shaped. Earlier that same day Devil Keith had been trusted with posting some important letters for a lovely mobster friend of theirs. Unfortunately, later that same night things got a wee touch ugly. Devil Keith had been leading a rather riotous conga line when he slipped and fell into a bathtub full of gin. The letters were still in his suit pocket as he forgotten to buy stamps. The letters were soaked through and consequently, completely ruined. This was despite Harry trying to dry them in front of a two-bar electric fire.

They were obviously important official forms. So Harry, in her tipsy wisdom, had quickly made up a new set of tax returns and posted them off. With hindsight she thought that she might have swapped a six for a zero, a three for a zero and a four for a zero. She also laughingly signed the forms, *"from a naughty, naughty mobster who likes to keep big dark secrets from the thieving government, shhhhsss"*.

Back to present day Hell...

"So, in short, Al Capone was arrested for tax evasion and jailed for a very long time. Devil Keith and I were put on a mafia hit list. Therefore, I don't think it would be safe for us to return. In fact, I

know it wouldn't be safe to return to that time period.

Taking all that into account; the best option is to go to Fachance's time. We can find her mother and hopefully speak with Roger too. We thought that Roger, as the common denominator, was probably the key to unlocking this problem and giving us all some closure. The Oracles thought so as well. Hence the need for a researcher." Harry finished her tale and wondered, not for the first time, whether she should write her memoir. Or, at the very least, apply for some reward money.

"Al Capone. Really? Tell me more, please." Gab was intrigued with Harry's mobster story. She had glossed over the facts when they were with the Oracles, plus Gab had been busy arguing then giving his hair it's hundred daily brushstrokes, so he had missed bits of the discussion. He had so wanted to visit Chicago during the prohibition but instead he had been assigned to Antarctica to settle a potential bloodbath. The famous 1931 shag and penguin uprising.

"No time for that. I say, no time. I know a top-notch researcher. Top notch, I say. I met her when I was researching my theft proof glasses and 'Talk Ability Scrolls.' Leave that to me. I say, leave that to me. I'll have to leave Dippit here. Can you make sure you keep her wrapped in the bubble wrap? The bubble wrap, I say. I've devised a basting type of cooling system so just keep that topped up. I say, topped up. If she wakes, can you tell her that'll be back soon? I say, soon.

Gab, can you give me a lift please? I say a lift." Stan put away his patchwork knitting bag, kissed Dippit's forehead and made to leave. He had started making essential baby items. So far, he had knitted a high-tech car seat, crocheted a pale green cot and was halfway through casting on to make a baby buggy. He was particularly pleased with his knitted baby monitor, but Dippit felt that a nuclear alarm siren linked in with the local radio station and a television network might be a bit much for the people of Falkirk to tolerate. Stan was still to be convinced.

THE DEVIL'S A HUNTING

CHAPTER TWENTY-THREE

Fifteen minutes later, when Gab and Stan returned with a small, stunning, busty blonde...

"Bowie, this is the team I've been talking about. I say, talking about. They really need your expert help. I say, expert." Stan nipped over to check on Dippit. She remained unresponsive but the coolant in her bubble wrap suit was keeping her temperature steady. The bubble wrap suit was designed to reduce the number of bruises that Dippit was collecting when she was fainting. Not weird at all. Nothing to look at here.

Stan had experimented with a number of liquids but had found that Irn Bru was the most effective cooling agent. He also found out that it was terrible to clean out of a carpet or rug but just the ticket for his current task, so the risk of the rusty stains was well worth it.

After introductions were made and the excited Bowie was promised a tour of Hell number one, they got down to work. They explained their dilemma and how the Time Scavenger worked.

"So, you're going to Fachance's time period? Ok. So, you'll need a detailed but memorable history of the city of Florence, Italy from 1501 to 1515. Something that Harry and Angel Gab can easily remember and hopefully easily rectify. If it comes to that.

You'll need a summary covering the key historical figures and the politics of the region. As it's the Renaissance period I would also suggest artists and sculptors, plus their key pieces of art should also be listed. Have I got the full brief? Is that correct?" Smiled a delighted Bowie.

They agreed and were so pleased they had someone who could take their jumble of needs and summarise it without being overwhelmed or think they were delusional. Bowie, not being particularly partial to screaming also helped their plight.

"Right. First off you'll need to blend in, so you need to look, sound, and act the part. Can you access costumes that would fit with the fashion of the time? Can you speak the language and adopt a local accent? Do you have money for lodgings and food and transport and possibly bribes?" Bowie was ticking items off on her fingers. She was itching to get started and couldn't believe her luck. No one would believe her story, but she was so pleased with the adventure that she didn't mind the secrecy and potential doubters. She was a wee bit annoyed that she wasn't allowed to bring her camera with her, but she could understand why there was a need for that rule.

Devil Keith volunteered to make the dresses, cloaks, boots and shoes at cost. He rushed off as they all agreed that they had to leave later that day or early the following day. Time was of the essence as Dippit was sporting a combover and was giving King Adrian a run for his money in the slenderness stakes.

Meanwhile, Harry and Gab confirmed that they could speak the language and could, if needed, fake a local accent that would fool the natives. A much improved Fachance wandered into the room during the discussion and asked to be updated. As an aside: her thumbs had grown in beautifully.

One update later...

"I'm coming too. I love Dippit and I want to help her. Plus, I want to see my old stomping ground and I literally speak like a native. I am an asset to the team and I hardly take up any space.

Not forgetting that, as the Horsewoman of Famine, I must help you maintain your strength and you know that you can't investigate on an empty stomach." Fachance looked around the room and was ready to stand her ground.

"*Come, please. You can come with me. Oh yes... you can, pretty lady.*" Gab was staring at the beauty in total awe. Her waist length, thick white hair shone with life and her lavender coloured eyes were so bright that they looked like they were spitting light into the darkness. Fachance was tall, slender and was swathed in a waif like innocence. The Angel was utterly hooked. Harry was rolling her eyes at the bat-winged buffoon.

Cue back story...

The previous year Fachance had been approached by a modelling agency and quickly signed to a lucrative contract. Despite her high cheekbones, wide smile, and clothes hanger body shape she was "*let go*" a few months later. Fachance was cagey about what had happened, but it was either due to her eating all of the snacks the models were permitted until the models were closer to starvation that usual. Or it could just as easily have been due to her force feeding the models until they were unrecognisably fat (AKA at a normal and healthy adult female weight) and they burst out of the designer's miniscule but exorbitantly priced creations. There was also a rumour that Fachance had repeatedly eaten all the expensive fruit scented make-up and had frequently projectile vomited into the carefully calibrated camera lenses. Harry, Dippit and Willing thought that it was possibly a combination of them all that had halted Fachance's skyrocketing career. They were probably right.

Gab was unaware of Fachance's peculiarities and just thought that he had never seen such a glorious sight. And he'd seen God with her full face of make-up on. Oh, yeah and he'd seen a fair few gorgeous sunrises too.

"*Yo... Angel Boy. Cooeee. Angel Boy. Anyone home. Gab you're dribbling on the floor.*" Harry was clicking her fingers in front of Gab's vacant face. She'd forgotten that Fachance rarely ever visited Hell number one and had never met Angel Gab before this.

"Pardon, Harry." Angel Gab absent mindedly muttered. He couldn't stop staring at the beauty.

"Oh, you have it bad, Angel Boy. You just called me Harry." Harry mischievously grinned and knew that there was some fun to be had with the uptight winged-one. Harry turned to wink at Dippit then everything felt sad again.

"What? No, I did not. Oh, do shut up. Ginger Girl." Flustered, Gab.

"Please, back to the business at hand," Karen couldn't understand what Gab was going on about. Fachance was just their Fachance: the unrelenting eating machine and the cause of many a ruination of their budget.

"So, in order to know how much detail you need can you tell me if you've been to Italy before and have you meddled with time before. What level of contingencies do I have to build into your plan?" Bowie perched her black rimmed glasses on her nose, pinned up her long blonde hair and was ready to take some detailed notes.

CHAPTER TWENTY-FOUR

S till in Devil Keith's office and design studio...

The stunning Fachance took a surprisingly long time to explain that yes, she had been to Italy before and no she had never knowingly meddled with the timeline. Well, no one who knew Fachance thought it was a surprisingly long tale, but Gab was perplexed by the number of details that were included and the frequency of meal and snack breaks.

Fachance confirmed that she had never interacted with any important historical characters or changed the outcome of wars or conflicts. She vehemently denied it, but she may have caused a few famines due to her voracious appetite and need to feed others. After all, she had eaten seventeen pork chops including the bones, three family sized Christmas cakes and four stuffed turkeys, including the giblets, during the first part of her story. There were also the twenty-two bowls of crème caramel whilst recounting the end of her tale.

Gab was so entranced with the beauty that he had tried to hand feed her some juicy, black grapes. Harry assured him that the tips of his fingers would re-grow quite quickly as Fachance had only nibbled them to the first joint. That also meant that Fachance liked him as normally she would have chewed through to the knuckle, wrist or possibly his elbow.

Devil Keith came bustling over with a sapphire blue, raw silk dress carefully draped over his arm. *"Harry, I thought even you'd look smashing in this gown. I had to let the seams out so no more pigging out at midnight for you. You'll also need an emergency pedicure so that your ragged toenails don't snag on the matching silk slippers. I'm sure I have a set of nippers for H.O.R.S.E. apostrophe S hooves in my toolbox. They might be up to the job otherwise it's the chainsaw... yet again.*" Keith finished with a sigh and a pitying look.

"*Oh Devil Keith, you've totally cracked it. Wow. That dress is so beautiful. I love it. I think it's one of your best creations, ever. Thank you so much. Oh, Fachance is coming as well. Can you make Gab and her some costumes too?*" Harry decided to ignore the "*even you*" and the "*pigging out*" comments as she was so impressed with the stunning outfit. The toenail comment was totally justified, and she so appreciated that Devil Keith had spelled out of the name of that wretched animal.

"*Erm, so Harry. Any issues with you going to Italy?*" Bowie was desperate for a Hell number one tour and wouldn't say no to a visit Italy as well. She was just waiting to be asked.

"*Harry, are we even allowed back into Italy?*" Devil Keith enquired as he pulled out his tape measure and started jotting down dress sizes and lengths. Fachance was such a pleasure to dress as she was so slender, and she made sure that she tucked in her napkin before every meal. There were no unsightly stains on her outfits, unlike the other philistines that he dressed. She also regularly nibbled on her own toenails so no grinder for her. No chainsaw either. Or flamethrower. Devil Keith was delighted and humming to himself.

"*What do you mean by 'allowed back'? Were you two deported? Can the Devil even be deported?*" queried a puzzled, Bowie. She feared that the Hell tour may be delayed by these new revelations.

"*Deported? Mmmm a topic for another day. Well in the past we have caused a smidgen of problems in Italy, but it wasn't really our fault. I think that sometimes we were framed.*" Harry was blushing and acting decidedly shady. She also tried to put her hand over

Devil Keith's mouth so he couldn't add any more to his telling comment.

"*Oh, do not tell me,*" sighed, Gab. He was being fitted for a scarlet tunic, hose, and a billowing white cotton shirt. He longed for his camouflage gear and sturdy Doc Martins. He wondered, not for the first time, why the Renaissance period was so flouncy and full of lace. Especially when you consider their lack of antiperspirant, poetry jams and need to be so handsy.

"*Ok, I won't. Bye.*" Harry turned to bustle away.

"*No... I mean tell me, but first...do I need a Falkirk Sewer to listen to this probable mayhem?*" Gab brushed back his hair and tied it with a black ribbon.

"*Erm...maybe? I'd get one if I were you. Make four, it's just as easy as making the one. It'll calm your nerves and it might stop you from pulling out any more of your fringe, Angel Boy.*" Harry was hedging her bets, but it's safe to say that Gab would need a few Falkirk Sewers to deal with this onslaught

CHAPTER
TWENTY-FIVE

Still in Devil Keith's office and design studio…

"Where to begin? Where to begin? Hmmm." Harry tapped her lip with her index finger. She had hoped to brush over her and Devil Keith's adventures, but Gab had the uncanny ability to make her tell the truth. Drat that Angel and his truth telling washing-powder. You couldn't even cut the labels off the back of your frocks. The washing-powder made you tell folks your real dress size and would never allow you to say that your clothes had shrunk in the wash. The impudent under-sink dweller.

"Begin? Begin? What do you mean begin? There's been more than one of your visits? More than one of your terrifying adventures?" Gab absentmindedly picked up a juicy grape and was soundly slapped by a famished Fachance. Harry held the story until Gab regained consciousness.

Harry and Devil Keith's ancient vacations…

"Maybe a few wee trips were had. A little adventure or two to stave off the boredom. Afterall, we have been around for a while and this place can be the tiniest little bit dull.

Right. Erm. Well, you know how Pompeii was buried by a volcano in 97AD." Harry let out a heavy breath. She crossed her fingers and sincerely hoped that Gab didn't know about Pompeii so she could slip past a lie or two. She was willing to argue that black was white with the Angel's grassing-up soap powder.

"Yes, Harry. I am aware of that catastrophic event. In fact, I would go as far as saying that most people are aware of that heinous occurrence so please uncross your fingers and desist from trying to construct an elaborate lie. My soap powder is particularly fragrant today.

Anyway, back to Pompeii. As I recall, it was Mount Vesuvius that violently erupted, and the subsequent river of lava buried the entire town. The plumes of smoke and ash were also particularly deadly. The unfortunate people were taken by complete surprise so they couldn't escape their fate. It was so fast. So unexpected that there were bodies frozen in everyday activities." Gab had a very bad feeling about this caper.

"Wellllll, Devil Keith and I may have had something to do with that occurrence. Just a little bit, mind you. You see, after a long day of hill walking we decided to do a wee bit of camping…" Harry could smell the Angelic soap powder getting ready to release a waft of "Summer Breeze" scent.

"Harry needed a hose down and a rub with some wire wool. She was sweating like a four-legged creature that cannot be named… for legal reasons. Or like a nun in a cucumber patch. I, however, was gently and quite beautifully glowing away to myself. Really quite nicely if I do say so." Devil Keith stopped hemming a magenta coloured, velvet cloak to add that essential nugget to the tale.

"Anyway, Devil Keith really wanted some barbequed goat. He was ravenous, and I was so concerned about him and his seismic stomach rumbles." Harry blustered.

"Really, Harry? Really? That's not how I remember it at all…" Devil Keith queried through a mouthful of tailor's chalk.

"Ahem. So we knocked an itty-bitty bit out of the top of Mount Vesuvius so that we could start a small fire. It worked a treat, so we may have knocked out a little more to speed up the whole cooking process. We were famished and the lava was barely leaking out at all. No more than a warm trickle. Promise." Harry gulped.

"I didn't even get any of the cooked goat. Turns out it was my third cousin, twice removed. Cousin Kevin. You know the one? The one that emigrated to Australia. He was on his holidays as it was his *gap year. Well, we couldn't really eat him. It's just not done, or so I've been told. That's the problem with having such a large family. You never know when, where or at what time your deoxyribonucleic acid will be sprackled all over the place."* Devil Keith tutted and shook his head in disappointment.

"Devil Keith, you know what DNA stands for? Really? I'm truly amazed. Totally gobsmacked. You still surprise me. How could you know that? I've seen you totally entranced by the movement of a woodpecker's beak. In fact, I've had to chase off at least four woodpeckers in the last week alone because you keep following their bizarre hypnotic suggestions.

Gab, it was as funny as fudge watching him eating an onion instead of an apple, but the robust sex with the immortal mountain gorilla was the stuff of nightmares. The things I had to ask them both to ensure that it was consensual sex was horrible. Just horrible. I thought having that conversation with Nora was going to be bad, but this dry run was gut wrenchingly revolting. I don't know if I'll ever be able to watch 'Gorillas in the Mist' ever again. And I really like Sigourney Weaver too." Harry shook her head and reluctantly put a copy of the movie *"Alien"* in her rubbish bin.

"Don't be such a girly wimp. I'll have to know, it was no 'wham, bang, thank you mam'. I'm now his newest friend on Facebook. Grant the gorilla's friend not Kevin's. Cousin Kevin was wearing denim short-shorts and suffering from a debilitating case of mange. Really quite off putting and I still haven't gotten over it despite it being hundreds of years ago." Devil Keith was screwing up his face when he accidentally swallowed three reels of thread. Harry was going to have to get him a couple of pints of melted lard and a rather large sewing needle. She'd check Roberto's extraction kit.

"Anyway, all of that is by the by. I'm no structural engineer. So how were we to know that the whole volcanic structure was going to collapse and rain lava down over the valley? We never, for a moment, thought that they wouldn't have some sort of early warning system or a beacon or some such thing. A chap in a tower with a horn: at the very least. They looked like they would have some procedures

in place. They were pretty cocky, afterall. Well from where we were they looked pretty cocky. Then they looked pretty scared then pretty screamy and finally quite ashy." Harry was spooning feeding Devil Keith some room temperature Vaseline as she had ran out of lard and cod-liver oil. Devil Keith was wriggling a large needle around in his boxer shorts and whispering *"here, thready, thready".* Well our Gab sincerely hoped it was a needle.

"Grant is your friend too? Sorry, I am struggling to erase that image... The volcano. We are discussing the volcano." Gab gave himself a couple of hard slaps to the face and had to hold Harry back from giving him a couple of roundhouse kicks. *"Right. Let me get this straight. You caused the destruction of a beautiful and culturally relevant town that had thrived since the seventh century BC because you wanted some mangy goat ribs? You did all that? For a snack?"* Gab was shaking his head and hiding a clump of his hair. The fringe was officially no more.

"Well, when you put it like that it sounds really bad. We did have a recipe for a particularly delicious barbeque rub, and we were ravenous. Well Harry was. I was gently peckish. We had walked all day and the lazy goat was just hanging around. I would go as far as to say that he was waiting on being roasted over a spit. I could see his acceptance of his fate. In fact, I would go as far as to say that he would have welcomed the extra warmth the barbeque offered. Well, until I realised it was mangy Cousin Kevin.

Plus, I am the Devil you know. I thrive on death and destruction. When will you people realise that?" Devil Keith unhelpfully added, whilst licking the Vaseline drenched spoon and humming in contentment.

"I do realise that you are the Devil for Hell number one. How could I ever forget? However, that incident was extreme, even for you. It was bad. Really bad! Many, many people died in a horrific way. It is famous for being a barbaric way to die. Burnt to a crisp or choking on ash. Tourists visit there just to see the crunchy remains.

However, it was a long time ago and I am sure that you both have learned your lesson. I take it that was the worst thing that you have done. Everything else is quite minor? You did learn your lesson? Yes?" Gab was on his second pint of Falkirk sewer, and he couldn't remember finishing the first pint. There was now a pronounced bald patch in the centre of his head, and he could feel his lips loosening.

CHAPTER
TWENTY-SIX

D evil Keith and Harry may not have learned their lesson...

"Wellll, about that. You know how the infamous Roman Coliseum was completed by Emperor Vespasian in 80 AD." Harry quickly added. She was engulfed in *"Summer Breeze"* scent so she reasoned that she either told Gab about their adventures or gave him her bank details.

"Yes. It was a glorious feat of ancient engineering and design. However, I could not support how it was used as many people and animals suffered due its pivotal role in the local entertainment scene. That being said: it looked positively stunning when it was completed and it continues to attract tourists to this very day. Ah, I am so not going to like where this is going. Am I?" Gab had started slurring his words and made an ill-fated decision to reach for another grape. Harry waited whilst Gab regained consciousness. Again.

Gab is nearly upright...

"Well, in 217 AD it was hit by lightning and in 1349 it was damaged by an earthquake. You could nearly say that it was cursed. Cursed I say. Spooky! Scary stuff! Going by the look on your face you're not really buying this, are you Gab?

Well, suffice to say... it was a bit on the wobbly side. Right up to early in the 19th century people were still pulling the Coliseum down so they could make other buildings with the loose stones. It was not *respected. Not at all.*

Now... well it's definitely not in mint condition; I think that we can all agree on that. Anyway, Devil Keith and I may have started that particular trend. Not entirely too sure though." Harry had her fingers, knees and eyes crossed as she spun that yarn.

"What trend? Natural disasters? Come on. Even you couldn't do that. Oh, surely not. That is just plain hubris." Scoffed Gab. He was struggling to follow the *"adventures"* and wasn't sure if it was the alcohol or just blessed denial. He also suspected that Harry was trying to bamboozle him by feeding him with bits and pieces of unnecessary information. Trying to subvert the truth telling washing-powder. The washing-power with the secret ingredients. It contained the tears and *"a certain look"* a mother makes when she is guilting the truth from her unsuspecting offspring.

"Eh no. Not the natural disasters but we did sort of use the Coliseum for a giant game of Jenga in 218 AD. I remember the date because Devil Keith had started a pink polka-dot toga trend and we were celebrating its successful launch.

Anyway, I think we might have started the craze of re-distribution of the stones and the tests of its structural stability. Well, the natural disasters didn't help either. However, we may have, ever so slightly, contributed to its current jiggly state. Just a teensy bit. A teeny, tiny bit. Hardly noticeable at all really. I think the lightening really did it in." Harry was holding her index finger and her thumb an inch apart. She was also getting mighty worried about Gab's profuse sweating and thought she might have heard him swearing. Actually, swearing quite a lot and with an imagination that rivelled Oracle Marjorie's.

"Harry, we never did get the royalties for inventing and publicising that game. We went to great lengths to get that game out and into the public domain. We employed a Town Cryer to shout about it for at least nine or ten months. Then there was the tournament we held. Damn liberty if you ask me." Devil Keith, again, unhelpfully added. Where was a mouthful of dress

making pins when you needed them?

"Right. Jiggly? You made it jiggly? Any more national monuments or Wonders of the World that you just happened to re-arrange, burn, or generally destroy? Did you pour weedkiller on the Hanging Gardens of Babylon by any chance? Were the petunias and begonias not to your liking? Did you prick your delicate little fingers on the thorn of a nasty, nasty rose? Did you then take umbrage at the nasty, nasty rose and salt the earth to make sure nothing else could grow there? Did you pave the glorious garden over to make an airport runway, a carpark or a skate park? Is that part of the origin of that song? Is the garden currently sitting under a local Primark by any chance?

Did you try to change the glorious Lighthouse of Alexandria from using a traditional fossil fuel lantern to using electricity? Was the original torch too dim to use as a spotlight for your vanity? Were you concerned that your audience would be unable to see your revolting gyrations? Did you hoist up a kite so you could harness the power of lightening to give extra pizzazz to the whole spectacle? Oh dear me, I presume the majestic lighthouse then went up in flames. You then danced around the blaze? Laughing and toasting marshmallows in the burning embers? Am I close?" Angel Gab sarcastically stated. He had no idea how close he was to the truth.

Harry opened her mouth, but Gab continued with his tumble of insults that may have not been insults at all.

"Did your pure and virginal little minds' take offense at the humungous Statue of Zeus? Was he too naked or stone coloured for your delicately wholesome tastes? Too Olympian to be endured by your sensitive eyes? Too offensive to your gentle sensibilities and fluffy wuffy feelings? Did you politely kneecap him, push him to the ground then grind down the odious statue? Then scatter the dust to the four winds or did you try to make the dust into a face pack? All the while, laughing hysterically and making up some type of victory high-five?

Did you sink Atlantis..." Gab was furious. He'd so wanted to see those ancient wonders but he'd nearly always been on duty or washing his hair.

"No, we did not sink Atlantis or go dancing under torchlight. Don't be facetious, you Angel, you. But you know how we all enjoy a wee flutter?" Harry knew that she had to confess to the next incident, but she wasn't entirely convinced that she and Devil Keith hadn't done some of the things that Gab had just accused them off. She did remember slathering on a particularly effective exfoliating, face pack.

"Yes. I know it is a common pastime around here." Sighed Gab. He wished that people would be less truthful around him. Shouldn't the folks in Hell delight in their deceit and just keep their gobs shut? He so needed to change his washing-powder.

"Well, Devil Keith bet me that I couldn't race around a Bell Tower before he downed four jugs of local red wine. They were really big jugs and the wine was really rank, so I thought I was onto a surefire winner. I bet two weeks' worth of laundry duty on the outcome of the race. I hated banging his smalls on the river rocks, but it was worth the risk. I thought it was a sure thing." Harry shuddered at the thought of going back to handwashing. She made a mental note to buy a new washing machine after Roberto had finished with all his chomping.

"Okay. You raced. Please continue with this fascinating tale." The third and fourth Falkirk Sewers were going down a treat, and Gab felt he could hear Harry just as well whilst lying nearer the floor.

"Well, it was around the 12th century and the Bell Tower was in this little town called Pisa. Don't know if you've ever heard of it?

Well, I didn't realise how strong the donkey was, so I happened to lose control. Only for a minute, mind you. It was enough for the silly ass to knock off the side of the tower. The donkey followed Devil Keith and knocked off the tower too. Well, that may have started the whole tilting process. It was only about 4 degrees off, so we scarpered and started the rumour that it was the soft ground that did it. The architect and builders were sacked, but I think we made the town famous so I don't think you can get onto us about that. We did a *good thing. In the long run.*" Harry put a plastic basin beside the downed Angel.

Gab had his head in his hands and was rhythmically rocking on the floor. "*So, let me get this straight. You ruined another building and probably caused craftsmen to lose their jobs? Their livelihood? Children to go hungry. It is not great, but it is nearly manageable... just. That is all? Please tell me that is all that I need to be concerned about.*" Gab pleaded.

"*That's all of it. Pinkie promise.*" Harry then mumbled, "*wliiwmlmy*". This translates to, "*well in Italy, anyway.*"

"*Oh, you wee, ginger fibber. What about the time you taught Emperor Nero how to play the lyre? He started that fire in Rome to get his hands on some prime real estate. The fire was only meant to cause a bit of smoke damage not take down the whole city. But nooooo.*

He was so busy making sure he was note perfect that he refused to listen to the screams for help. I think you contributed to that too. If you hadn't insisted on total perfection, then ancient Rome might have survived that act of arson. You were a fierce taskmaster. I think you made Nero cry a couple of times, so he was too scared and scarred to stop playing in order to deal with the carnage," Devil Keith helpfully added and raked through a box of buttons. Gab's shirt was coming on a treat.

Harry couldn't fathom how Devil Keith's mind worked. He could barely understand how to use a kettle, but he could sew the most amazing items of clothing. He couldn't work out that he wasn't a conspirator for Hell number three, but he could reason out a Roman catastrophe and correctly allocate blame. He was a weirdo, but not in a good way.

"*And to think... I thought Devil Keith was **always** the liability in your clodhopping duet. I was under the misconception that you were the one that stopped the worst of Devil Keith's antics. Ginger Girl, you **are** the liability. You **are** the clodhopper.*

Are you finished now? Please tell me that I do not have to listen to any more of your confessions. Where is Devil Keith off to now?" Gab was like a sailor on shore leave drunk, and he had lost all his diplomacy skills. A common occurrence in Hell number one.

"I am not a liability. You take that back, Angel Boy. And for your information Devil Keith is away measuring Roberto. He said something about needing to make a new coat. Oh, now that I think about it; the coat wasn't for Roberto but it was gonna be made from Roberto. So there. Take that you overgrown budgie.

He also failed to tell you that he was responsible for the Great Fire of London. Devil Keith thought his treacle scones needed baked for longer and he forgot to take them out of the oven. So, you see. It's not all on me. You… Angel Boy." Harry crossed her arms in the huff.

"Right. You, me, Fachance and Devil Keith are heading to Florence. I cannot risk leaving Devil Keith here. Nor can I leave you unattended. Karen, can you please look after Roberto for me? There's stool-softeners under the sink if you need them. Bowie, over to you. I wish you luck in trying to make this plan fool proof or should I say 'Ginger Girl' proof.

Ginger Girl, can you please retrieve Devil Keith and tell him the news? I think I may have vomited inside this bean bag." Gab staggered and headed for the kitchen sink.

CHAPTER TWENTY-SEVEN

S till, still in Devil Keith's office and design studio…

Bowie was shocked at the amount of chaos two beings could cause then just dismiss as irrelevant. She was amazed and envious at the sights they would have seen, the places they had visited and the people they had met. She would have adored to have seen some of those adventures, but she knew it wasn't to be. She could well understand why the Oracles were furious at the loss of the precious Time Viewer. That device would have been the ultimate tool in any researcher's arsenal. To witness history unfold without any bias or interference or interpretation or agenda. Just plain facts: the applications were truly limitless.

Although despondent she decided to live vicariously and ensure that the team were well prepared although being *"Ginger Girl"* proof may have been too much of an ask. Being Devil Keith proof was also totally out of the question.

The plan…

Karen decided to stay in Hell number one in order to keep the place going. She also agreed to look after the munching Roberto and keep his bits *"running properly."* She was also keen to use Bowie's ample skills to start the search for the Big Bang Runes. Karen wasn't too optimistic as they had over four billion years of history to rake through.

Dr Riel was staying in Hell so that he could look after Dippit, and that would allow Stan the time to attempt to find a cure for the fainting. Just in case the team was unsuccessful in their quest. Dr Riel also had another ceiling to fix and an unprofessional maintenance crew to bribe. They had started to giggle every time he came near them.

The four man/woman team decided to split into two small teams so they could cover more ground. Gab thought the less time spent in Renaissance Florence the better. In theory, the least amount of time spent would equate to less opportunities they had of damaging the city, the people, and the timeline. That was the hope anyway.

Harry and Angel Gab had rote learned the necessary history and when questioned they were word perfect. Bowie had done a marvellous job despite the considerable time constraints and distractions. Devil Keith kept insisting that she devise a method of categorising his treasures instead. Gab skelpt him about the head with a soggy beanbag and Devil Keith suddenly realised that he no longer had any treasures. None at all.

The small teams had decided to take on the persona of wealthy merchants so that they could travel around the city with relative ease. Karen had packed approximately three months' worth of imperishable foods into sturdy leather cases. She thought the salted meats, sacks of rice, bags of grains, jars of honeyed plums, and barrels of wine-soaked fruits might stave off a Florentine famine for a while. They had bags of coins for additional daily food stuffs, their lodgings, travel, and enough funds for servants. There were extra coins in case they needed to offer bribes for information regarding Roger's whereabouts. The lying cheating cretin. Harry just took over the typing and is being wrestled away from the author's laptop...

CHAPTER TWENTY-EIGHT

K aren's executive suite...

Gab, Fachance, Devil Keith and Harry gathered around their substantial stack of luggage. Devil Keith had provided them all with enough outfits for a three-week mission; hence his own separate mountain of large suitcases. Gab had then removed ten pairs of Devil Keith's stilettos from his one suitcase, as they were not in keeping with the time period. Devil Keith's tantrum was so horrific that Gab feared for the safety and stability of the Great Wall of China. However, Gab stuck with the mission boundaries and argued the toss with the pouty toddler. Gab believed that he had won that discussion. Poor deluded fool.

Devil Keith then snuck in another seventeen pairs of shoes but he had to spread them throughout the pile of luggage as he nearly did his back in when he lifted his cases. He thought that Harry, and her abysmal lack of interest in fashion, only really needed clothing for a week so he put in one change of outfit for her and another four hats for himself. He reasoned that she would enjoy the view of his striking figure as he bounded about Florence.

Fachance and Harry kissed Dippit's cold forehead and stroked her hair. That was their promise to her that they would do their best and try to find a cure. Stan and Karen held each of them in a tight hug and reminded them to return as quickly as possible. And to keep safe.

Gab tentatively held the Time Scavenger, with a strand of Fachance's hair, in the air. The Scavenger looked like an exceptionally large, sharp bladed hacksaw and Gab had insisted that his cloaks all had pockets big enough to hold it. It was not leaving his sight. He was not getting stuck in Florence with that pair of toerags. He carefully cut through the air and blinked. Hard.

The city of Florence was teeming with life and vitality. The small teams gasped as they had forgotten how wonderful it all was. The sensory overload was staggering and exciting and fabulous. The cries of the street venders as they imaginatively boasted and sold their fresh breads and pastries was delightful. The antics of the flamboyant poets as they competed to be heard above the din was hilarious. This was combined with the chipping of chisels through creamy sandstone and imposing blocks of marble. The unveiling of masterpieces and the creation of such awe-inspiring beauty was everywhere.

The tangy smells wafting from barrels of juicy black olives, crates of ripe glistening oranges, the strings of drying garlic, trays of warm breads and the coils of fresh onions was tantalising on the tongue. This was tempered by the odours billowing from the heaps of rotting horse manure and the barely washed towns folk.

The early evening sun gently bathed the buildings in warm light and added to the sensations of romance and love. The choking dust, fluttering brightly coloured clothes lines and clouds of flies added to the overall atmosphere of the bustling metropolis.

The intrepid team nodded to each other then climbed through the light infused, slice in time. They were going hunting.

"I hope they keep safe. I don't want anything to happen to

them. Stan, I had so wanted you to go with them but I agree that you can't. Gab has his work cut out for him keeping them all in check. Now we just have to sit and wait it out. Anyone for a cuppa and a chocolate biscuit? I would murder for a custard cream biscuit." Karen was downhearted and worried as she walked off to make a snack.

CHAPTER TWENTY-NINE

K aren's executive suite...a few minutes later...

Bowie had just left, with a flask of urine infused tea clutched in her hand, to meet the notorious Neville. She had heard such delightful stories of Neville's outstanding bravery and she couldn't wait to play with the Hounds of Hell puppies. There had been another two litters added to the pack, so Carmen and Neville now had the support of two sets of new parents. Plus, Neville's little runt of the litter Hugo had new playmates in the form of the delightfully delinquent Olive and the rambunctious Rolly. Bowie had packed a Spanish phrase book, iron gauntlets, titanium chew toys and a six-pack of pork-scratchings so she could experience the whole enchilada.

An unexpected visitor...

"*Loo, loo. Out of my way. I need a pee. Oh, now.*" Harry danced and dashed past a shocked Karen, Stan, and Dr Riel. Dippit remained unconscious and propped up in the middle of the room.

"*Shirt, shirt. I need a shirt. Out of my way,*" a naked and extremely buff Gab galloped past an even more shocked Karen, Stan, and Dr Riel. He bolted out of the room and belted towards Devil Keith's workroom.

"*Wow, did you see his skin? He positively glows. I've never seen anything quite like it. Do you think he normally hides all that hotness with a good dollop of foundation?"* Karen was very tempted to follow the streaking Angel and offer him a wee dab of concealer for his muscular nether regions.

"Karen, I'm not really the person to have this conversation with but yes, he is a fine specimen of a man. A very fine specimen indeed," Dr Riel decided that the swing required some urgent attention. He needed to keep his woman occupied and in lust.

Ten minutes later and a more settled Harry and Gab came strolling back into Karen's suit of rooms. Unfortunately, Gab was fully dressed… and much calmer. Afterall you can't win them all. Sorry Karen…Dr Riel bribes better than you do.

Update…

Harry and Gab had only been away for five minutes, in Dr Riel and Karen's time period, but they had been in Florence for a full day, a night and this was the following morning for them. Gab explained that on arrival in Florence, he had partnered with Harry so that left the more sensible Fachance with the lunatic Devil Keith. Gab reasoned that it was safer to divvy up Harry and Devil Keith so that Florence could escape the worst of their joint shenanigans.

Gab and Harry had spent their first day unsuccessfully trolling the markets, hostels, churches and taverns for any signs of the illusive Roger. They had left Devil Keith and Fachance to find them lodgings, unpack the cases, set up the rooms, secure the foodstuffs and hire the necessary serving staff.

A slightly disappointed Harry and Gab had returned to their villa in need of a hearty meal, a warm bath, and a stiff drink or two. Unfortunately, Fachance had either eaten it herself, or distributed all of their three-month food supply to the poor and needy. Gab thought she was really generous but slightly misguided in her compulsive need to help others. Harry was furious as she knew that Fachance had probably eaten more than ninety-five percent of the supplies as there were suspicious teeth marks on the remains of the empty barrels of salted pork.

In Harry's opinion, Fachance was less generous and more of an insatiable gorger. Where was Willing's magnificent mallet when you needed it?

Fachance had also either spent or given away all of their money so there were no servants in the house or wood for heating the bath water. Plus, they had also lost the ability to pay to re-stock their depleted food supplies. Again, Gab chose the path that put Fachance in the very best light. He proclaimed her to be as kind and charitable as she was beautiful. Harry kept quiet. He'd learn and he did.

Poor deluded Gab had woken up the following day to find that Fachance had snuck in during the night and stolen all of his clothes. She then sold her spare clothes, all of his clothes and their curtains, in order to buy a hearty breakfast or six. Harry and Devil Keith had hidden an emergency set of their clothing under their pillows as they knew Fachance of old. This *"cute theft"* episode was the reason for the gorgeous streak of naked male flesh. As aside, who knew that all Angels slept in the buff?

Gab was visiting Hell number one in order to collect more money, gather some food, pinch some of Devil Keith's clothing and commandeer a pair of thick curtains. He knew he wouldn't be able to sleep with the sun coming in so early in the morning. He also needed a fair few padlocks, several lengths of heavy-duty chains and, if at all possible, a few reinforced steel Safes to keep the new luggage, groceries and soft furnishings secure. That would help keep the gentle Fachance at bay, as although he knew she was caring, kind and exquisite he also now knew that she had no impulse control; none whatsoever. The gorgeous little giver. The heavenly hostess and other such nonsensical claptrap had also been bandied about by the smitten and delusional Gab.

Harry had used the excuse of needing to collect some of Devil Keith's clothing to come home for a much needed pee, a hot soapy shower, a squirt of deodorant and some fresh under pants. She had forgotten just how dirty and smelly history was.

The leather, cotton and wool clothing was rough, disgusting and desperately needed a blast of scented Febreze. She was also slightly sunburnt as Devil Keith had ditched all of her factor sixty sunscreen in favour of some of his hideous, sparkly platforms and grotesque hats. She's a ginger so the sunscreen was essential. The team had also forgotten to pack a six pack of 2 ply toilet roll. A rookie mistake if ever there was one. Tut, tut.

Karen perched her full cup of tea and plate of custard creams on her knee then requested a more detailed catch up. Plus, any updates to their proposed plan.

The catch up …

*"We might not have found that rotter Roger, but we did meet Michangelo Buonarroti. **The** Michangelo. The artist. It was so exciting. He's an astonishing man and not at all how he's portrayed in the history books that Bowie showed us. I would go as far as to say that he's the life and soul of the party. We found him in a sleazy tavern where he was standing on a wobbly table whilst reading some of his rather racy poetry. He mimed the rude bits and used different voices and accents when describing his critics. It was so fudging funny that I sprayed red wine all over Gab's new green tunic. Angel Boy wasn't best pleased and started to huff, but Michangelo thought it was an absolute hoot.*

Gelo, that's his pet name. Well, pet name that only his closest friends are allowed to use. He said he would be delighted if we used it. Isn't that amazing? Gelo has some really brilliant stories. Did you know that his nose had been badly broken when he was an apprentice? He's going to tell us all about it later. Seemingly it's one for the history books.

Talking of which… the history books got other bits wrong too. They portrayed him as an unattractive man and the self-portrait we saw prior to going to Florence supported that. But to be honest I hardly noticed his looks as he is so cool, charismatic, charming, and unbelievably magnanimous. He also does the most amazing caricatures and insists that people keep them, totally free of charge.

If it weren't for the urgent need to help Dippit I would have sat watching and listening to him all day. He's phenomenal. Just phenomenal.

I wish you could meet him. In fact, now that I think about it, I think we should all go and meet him after we get Dippit better. Talking of which, we need to get back and make sure we still have a pot to pee in. Did you like that one? No?

Karen, if you want I can get you an autograph for your collection. I'll ask him if you can call him Gelo too. Wish us luck and we hope to be back in a couple of days." Harry was dripping wet but smelling so much fresher, so she was ready to return to their adventure. Gab was back to his gorgeous, tailored self and strenuously denied ever being in the huff. He was just resting his bottom lip on his chin.

Karen and Dr Riel were big fans of Michangelo's work, so they were delighted at the prospect of meeting him; especially as he sounded like a right character. They excitedly spoke about having a joint caricature drawn, then they started making some holiday plans. Whilst they were distracted, Gab stole their packet of biscuits and rammed them into his mouth.

Back to Florence they go.

CHAPTER THIRTY

K aren's executive suite…

A slightly panicked and exasperated Harry returned five minutes later. She explained that nearly two weeks had passed in Renaissance Florence. They still hadn't found the dastardly Roger and they were losing all hope. Plus, to make matters worse they had completely lost Devil Keith. She wondered if he had, somehow, returned to Hell number one and was hiding out with Karen and Dr Riel. Last time she saw him he was heading off to see Michangelo's studio then popping out for a pint of ale. He had promised to be back in a couple of hours but that was nearly ten days ago. Harry was frantic with worry.

"Who or what is a Michangelo?" queried a puzzled Dr Riel. He looked at Karen and hoped she knew what Harry was talking about. Karen shrugged her slender shoulders.

"You're joking, right? Please tell me you're joking. He's famous. He's also a sculptor, painter, architect and poet of the High Renaissance. I spoke about him during my last visit here. You're huge fans of his work. You actually used the words 'fans of his work' before I went to Florence. You wanted an autograph or a sketch for your office wall. I was going to ask him if you could call him Gelo. You were planning a holiday just so you could meet him. Ringing any bells?" Harry hoped they were joking and really didn't appreciate their attempts at humour.

Harry was dusty, dirty, stressed and bone tired. Plus Fachance was continuing to steal, eat and sell off all their belongings so that was causing quite a lot of arguments. Gab was shocked when he found Fachance biting the padlocks off the cases and politely chewing through the steel Safe doors. Harry thought that he'd maybe worked out just how *"kind"* Fachance really was. Harry had taken to reminding Gab, on a daily basis, that Fachance was the Horsewoman of Famine. And as such she was just following her nature. Harry actually used the word horse in a sentence, so Angel Gab was beginning to realise just how import this daily reminder was. Harry was also realising just how much work Willing did to keep Fachance contained. Poor Willing deserved a medal.

"Sorry, Harry. I've never heard of him. Can you tell us more just in case we've forgotten him? I'm not as young as I use to be so it might just have slipped out of the old noggin," Dr Riel was such a sweetheart and wanted to ease Harry's worries.

"Well, according to the notes I memorised. Michangelo sculpted 'David'. A seventeen-foot-high statue made from Carrera Marble. He created it between 1501 and 1504. The statue was based on the noble, beautiful and heroic biblical figure that defeated the huge Goliath. The statue's a symbol of Florentine Independence. It's really, really famous. I can't stress that enough." Harry was pacing and wondered if this was how normal people dealt with her misadventures.

"No, nothing. I'm so sorry. Can you tell us some more? He sounds absolutely fascinating," Karen offered Harry a biscuit to help calm her nerves.

"Michangelo was only twenty-six when he started sculpting 'David', and Gelo is twenty-eight just now so he should be knee deep in marble dust. That's why Devil Keith wanted to tour his studio.

Anyway, back to 'David'. Sculpting something like that was an amazing achievement. He's famous for saying that he 'released David from the stone.' Does that help at all? Stir a memory?" Harry was becoming increasingly desperate as she munched her way through a full packet of chocolate hobnobs then spat out the wrapper. Harry began to experience a horrible, horrible feeling. Where was Devil Keith and what had he done to change history in such a drastic way?

"*I'm so sorry, Harry. We just haven't heard of that person. Are you sure that he was famous? That well known?*" Karen questioned.

"*He painted the Sisten chapel? He did the murals on the ceiling? In the Vatican, around 1508 to 1512?*" Harry was frantically grasping at straws. She then mimed painting the Vatican. Well Karen thought she was miming painting the Vatican, or she might have been having a seizure. The Hell number one games nights all resulted in at least one stroke, a sizeable seizure, a pregnant donkey and a very satisfying punch up.

"*The Vatican?*" Dr Riel looked confused.

"*No, no, no surely not the Vatican too? You must know about the Vatican. It's in Rome? Where the Pope lives? The really famous guy in the white suit and pointy-ish hat? He talks about love and forgiveness? He also smiles and waves a lot from his balcony? He has a car with a massive sunroof? That Vatican.*" Harry was pacing and pulling at her bedraggled hair.

"*Sorry, Harry. Yes, we know where and what the Vatican is. We were just pulling your leg. Trying to lighten the mood a little.*

I have to say though. It wasn't some chap called Michangelo who painted the Sisten Chapel. I think some stone mason's apprentice just slapped some whitewash on the ceiling and walls. It's not that famous and I don't know anyone who's visited it. Was the chapel meant to have murals on it?" Karen shrugged and looked at Dr Riel for confirmation.

"*Yes, it was. They're amazing, Karen. Brilliant. Stunning. Really famous. Well, that confirms it. I have to find Devil Keith and sort out what he's done now. I think Gab may have a point. We really are a menace to ourselves and others.*" Harry sighed and readjusted her bra straps.

A blustering Harry left Hell number one to post yet more missing person scrolls and Karen wondered how she had managed to get the Time Scavenger from Gab's pocket.

CHAPTER THIRTY-ONE

Karen's executive suite...

Another few minutes went by then Harry returned to Hell number one.

"Do you two spend all of your time drinking tea and eating chocolate biscuits? Don't you have work to go to?" Harry barked then rubbed her tired eyes.

"Harry, pet. You have visited us three times in less than an hour and each time you pinched our biscuits, so we keep having to get more. You're the one that keeps having all the tea breaks." Huffed, Karen. Hiding the much-coveted chocolate eclairs in between the couch cushions.

"Sorry, this time travelling thingy is difficult to negotiate and exhausting. Have you heard from my Bub? Scrub that. I've been away from him for weeks and I miss him so much, but he's only been away for a day or so. Hardly had any time to miss me or fall in love with a cat.

Oh well. Right time for my report." Smiled the weary and beaten down Harry. *"I'm pleased to say that we found Devil Keith, but he's so hungover that he can't string two words together just now. He had been on a massive bender with Michangelo, and I mean Massive with a capital Mmmm. I found him hanging upside down from a washing line drunkenly singing to a pair of turtledoves. He thought he was recoding a video. Seemingly pigeons record sound but doves can record sound and images. The birds flew away before I could check the footage.*

Anyway, I think he may have broken the sculptor or done something to him. But I'm not sure, so I thought if I gave you an update then I could possibly fathom out some of Devil Keith's antics and make sure we've not fatally broken history. Again." Harry fell into the couch and Karen rubbed her aching feet.

Harry explained that due to Devil Keith's interference the gregarious character, that was Gelo, was no more. Michangelo had sworn off drinking alcohol, eating sweets and messing around with loose women. He had changed into a miserly, grouchy man. It was so sad. He had lost his happy, chubby tummy and was now less than 100 pounds. And that was when he was dripping wet, and we mean dripping. Sodden, sopping, soggy...you get the picture.

His broken nose was so much more noticeable now, and it turns out that he wasn't handsome. Not at all. He had transformed into an unhappy genius living in squalid conditions and barely changing his rancid clothing. He was positively monk like; only eating and drinking for fuel rather than for pleasure. There were no more wine laden afternoons in the local pub, and he had banned pork scratchings and pickled eggs from the menu as he believed they were too decadent. It was such a shame. He was melancholy, solitary and no longer answering to his pet name.

Instead of naughty prose he now only spoke about anatomy and dissecting fresh cadavers. He no longer did cartoons or impromptu paintings in the local taverns. Rather, he was setting fire to his drawings to hide his talent. That way no one could copy him.

"It's just awful but I suppose that it's closer to how Bowie originally described him, so that's something. Positive in a weird way. I feel so sorry for Gelo." With that Harry slouched further into the sofa and searched down the side of the cushions for any stray hoola-hoops. She was particularly keen on the cheese and

onion potato snack, but she was so hungry that she's even eat the beef variety. That is the true definition of hunger.

"Harry, that's awful but who is this poor chap and how does he feature in your search for Roger? You seem to be the only one who knows and cares about him." Karen queried and patted Harry's shoulder.

"Karen you still don't know who Michangelo is? How important he is? How can that be?" the exhausted Harry wiped away a solitary tear. *"I thought the timeline was repaired. Off to do a bit more of the old historical repairs then."*

It was only when she left that Karen discovered the missing eclairs. Bloody crocodile tears!

CHAPTER THIRTY-TWO

Karen's executive suite…

"Right, before I start. Who is Michangelo and what is he famous for?" Harry winced and held her breath. It must be all sorted now she thought, hoped and prayed.

"Oh, oh I know this one. He's a sculpture and a painter. He's famous for painting the Sisten Chapel and carving the hunky 'David'. Grumpy old bugger seemingly, but really talented." Cooed, Karen, lowering her hand.

"Yes! Yes! Yes! I think it's fixed." Harry began dancing around the room and kissing Karen on the forehead. *"You clever, clever, wonderful woman."*

Harry explained that since her last visit to Hell number one she had managed to gather more information from the pitiful Devil Keith. It turned out that Michangelo had indeed gone drinking with Devil Keith and due to his colossal hangover Gelo had sworn off all forms of decadency and sin. Hence the awful monk-like behaviour that was just like the history books originally described him. She had also found out that Devil Keith had totally wrecked one of Michangelo's favourite models. Hence Karen and Dr Riel's prior lack of knowledge about Michangelo and his spectacular creations.

What Devil Keith did to history…

The artist's model, who had been accidentally knobbled by

Devil Keith, was being used to create the famous statue David. Devil Keith, in his wisdom, had been teaching said model to juggle one ripe apple when the model pulled his hamstring. No one's entirely sure how that was even possible. Harry had tried all of the moves used in juggling, and the most she received was a couple of balls to the chin.

As Michangelo was currently working on carving the statue David's buttocks he was less than pleased with this set back. In a fit of rage he had said that he was planning on taking a sledgehammer to the block of marble. Harry and Gab fought to save the statue, so they had persuaded Devil Keith to stand in for the model (quite literally, as it turns out) so Michangelo could continue with his chiselling.

Devil Keith tried to argue that his flashing green blue eyes, surfer blond hair and gorgeous dimples would be the better option, but Michangelo slapped him and told him that *"his David"* would never have dimples not even on his firm bottom.

"So, if you look closely at the statue David you'll see Devil Keith's bum cheeks there." Harry had no intention of ever looking that closely. Yuck, yuck. Thank you very much. The identical twin thing was kinda lost on her at times. Well, all of the time to be fair.

"Well, that's quite some story. How about Roger? Has he made an appearance? How are Gab and Fachance doing?" questioned Karen.

"I was dreading you asking that. Ah, well that's not so good. Roger is still as elusive as ever and to make matters worse I've now lost Gab and Fachance. A few days ago Gab was calming down the local market vendors. Fachance had just engaged in some of her legendary haggling and was adding a colander, a ricer, two whisks and a pizza paddle to her saddle..." Harry was clearly traumatised by her sister and her antics.

"Oh, I've seen Fachance haggle. It was brutal. I had to lie down in a darkened room for a fortnight after that. Those poor, poor vendors. What were they thinking? Going up against Fachance?"

Karen was wincing at the memory.

"Yeah, me too. It makes me shudder. I've heard well substantiated rumours that it was Fachance's haggling that started the Napoleonic wars. Something about arguing about paying less for trousers because he was so short. However, despite her many faults we have to agree that her introducing G.O.D. to hostess trolleys was a belter. Especially with the price Fachance managed to negotiate for the appliance.

Anyway, where was I? So, after Gab cooled the situation down he went to check on Fachance and her purchases. Well, he walked out after finding Fachance eating the corner off a painting by Leonardo da Vinci. The famous Mona Lisa and the corner with the wombats dressed as court jesters. You know the one? Seemingly that's the real reason for Mona's smile. Well, Gab actually raised his voice to Fachance when he found her 'snacking' and going in for more.

I think it must have registered with Fachance just how upset and disappointed Gab was, as she ran out after him. I haven't seen them since.

To be honest, I think I'm really over this whole-time travelling lark. It's exhausting keeping track of things and not that exciting. I'll give it another go, then I think I might have to bite the bullet and head to Willing's time. It's looking like the more sensible idea despite the mafia hit and machine guns." Harry dragged herself out of the comfortable sofa and started to leave.

"What wombats?" Karen stage whispered.

CHAPTER THIRTY-THREE

Karen's executive suite…

Harry's back again. Hopefully for the last time as Karen's nearly out of biscuits and her tea's getting cold.

"Right, before I start. Who is Michangelo and does the Mona Lisa have wombats?" Harry dragged in a breath, scrunched up her face and held her body tight. Getting ready to wince at the answer.

"He's an artist and no she doesn't have wombats." Dr Riel happily confirmed.

"Oh that's such a relief. Yeah. I think everything is back in its rightful place. I'll be back soon. Just a couple of loose ends to tidy up first. And the small matter of a crotchety Devil to unchain." Harry did her uncoordinated happy dance around the couch, hit her shin, and then nipped away.

A few minutes later…

Gab, Harry, Fachance and Devil Keith plopped back into Karen's room. They then made a mad dash for the door whilst shouting about needing showers, a pee, some lice cream and a nice potted plant.

Thirty minutes later and the travellers returned. Smelling a good deal better and scratching a good deal less than before.

"Sooooo. Don't keep us in suspense…" Karen merrily produced her talking stick aka blue felt-tipped pen and handed it

to an exhausted Harry.

Yet another update...

Harry explained that Michangelo was happy, or as happy as he was ever going to be, with David's new buttocks. He was no longer going to take a hammer to the famous statue, so that was a relief. Harry surmised that the paintings for the Sisten Chapel were back on track too. Karen confirmed that the Sisten Chapel was not currently covered in a coat of whitewash and it did indeed look smashing.

On the subject on the wombats. Leonardo da Vinci had lopped the corner off the Mona Lisa painting, so the mystery of her smile was back to being entrenched in the history books. The imprint of Fachance's choppers were merrily consigned to the nearest bin. However, Leo so enjoyed the antics of the little wombats that they were going to feature in their very own da Vinci collection titled, *"The Cute Cube Poopers and how to dress them for success"*. Karen made a mental note to find that lost collection so she could balance the grocery budget and fix her bloody ceiling.

Wait just a cotton-picking minute... how did da Vinci get those wombats when the first Europeans didn't land in Australia until 1606? Those fudging Oracles and their scavenging ways. The minxes!

Devil Keith was currently *"off the bevy"*, as he still felt a little bit *"sloshy"* inside and a wee bitty *"bruisey"* outside. He had also learned how to do air quotes so that was...nice? Devil Keith's sobriety wasn't likely to continue so Karen decided to take her chance and get her Wicked Stepmother costume measured and ordered up. Plus, she had to be quick as Gab looked like he'd need a few of his outfits adjusted as he was less Angel-like and more Angelcake-like. The authors are trying, and failing miserably, to say that Gab was now slightly plumper than usual.

"What about them?" Karen pointed over her shoulder.

"*Oh they're 'in love'. I just hope they don't have any children 'what' with his 'wings' and 'her' appetite they're likely to make 'a' plague 'of' attractive locusts. Put 'her' down or get a fudging room. Not my 'room' ya pervs.*" Yep, the air quotes were going "to" be Devil Keith's "thing" from now on.

Gab stopped gnawing the face off Fachance long enough to mumble, "*spare room? Spareribs? Spare tyre?*" Then the nauseating fawning re-started as Gab and Fachance flopped around, heading for the office door. Stan physically stopped their salacious escape and told them to take a seat as they might be needed. Actually there was a surprising amount of graphic and repetitive swearing squashed into that one-sided conversation. The horny hounds did take a fudging seat and sort of behaved themselves, although the blanket they were hiding under gave them away. It looked like three feral ferrets and a couple of circus clowns were practicing their line dancing routine under there. And the noises!

"*Just in case you haven't noticed all the face sucking and the stripping. Although you'd have to be blind, deaf and lucky to miss that floorshow, they've made up. In amongst the spit swapping I think they said that they had decided to start a cookery book range. The books will be flavoured so you can eat them right off the shelf. I don't think they've thought it through, but it should save a few art galleries becoming an all you can eat buffet, so I think we just let them go for it.*" Harry tutted but was secretly happy for them. It saved ruining two other families.

"*Did you find Roger?*" Dr Riel enquired and turned his back on the snogging pair.

"*Yes. Yes, I fudging well did.*" Harry scrunched up her face and began beathing heavily.

CHAPTER THIRTY-FOUR

R oger's revelations…

Harry had found Roger in a back-street brothel with a couple of well-used, drunken wenches haphazardly piled on his knee. She was just glad that she rocked up when she did, or she might have witnessed a truly horrific and potentially erotic performance. For erotic also read disturbing, sickening, horrendous and vomit-inducing. You get the picture.

Harry was livid when she roughly grabbed the disease-soaked wenches and tossed them to onto the filthy floor. She then viciously grabbed the startled and blustering Roger by the ear. She dragged his complaining ass from the tavern, diverted him through a rather busy pigsty and threw him to the ground. She pulled out a lethal looking sword and held it a *"baw-hair"* away from his right eyeball.

"Right you malingering, geriatric gobshite, where have you been? And no lies or I'll pop your lying eyeball from its lying socket. You fudging liar. You serial adulterer. You…. liar, you!" Harry used the point of the sword to press on Roger's tear duct.

"Harlot? Harlot is that you? It can't be. Is your mum with you?" A startled Roger gasped.

"Yes it is. And no she isn't, so don't pretend to care. You traitorous old tart. Now start talking and it better be good. I want to know why you keep abandoning your wives and children. Why you keep breaking up families. You fudging monster. Where have

you been?" Harry growled and gave Roger a quick kick to the ribs then twisted his permanently protruding nipples.

Roger talked and talked then talked some more.

CHAPTER THIRTY-FIVE

Karen's room...

"*Well it turns out that I have daddy issues. Who knew? Karen, please don't answer that. Anyway, the main daddy issue being that I want to viciously beat him to death then revive him and do it all over again. Finding him and getting some answers has helped a bit, but he's still a silly cookie-bun.*

Well, the reason for the 'a long line of escorts' noted as his previous backstory is because he's one eighth incubus so technically they are escorts. Ancient male escorts. Unlike a full incubus, Roger doesn't necessarily need souls to survive but they help to extend his pathetic life. He takes a tiny amount of the person's soul during each 'coupling'. But it does mount up over time hence the use of the brothels when he has a perfectly lovely wife at home. Well that's what he said anyway. The sorry excuse for a man. That's also why he left Morag when I was in my teens. He said that he 'didn't want to risk his beautiful druid priestess' any longer. He knew he had been slowly killing her but stayed anyway. He should have left before we both became so attached to him, but I think he convinced himself that he really did care about us.

He then went onto use the same excuse for loving and leaving Dippit's mum. He left Helena a lot quicker in the soul-stealing process, so Dippit had less memories to supress. She was spared from seeing her mam fade away and nearly die. I'm glad of that. It's helped to preserve her innocence.

Roger was cagey about the number of women he's 'loved' and left hanging, but I think it's safe to say that I probably have a veritable squad of half siblings out there. He didn't even register my feelings of disgust over his behaviour. He said that it's his nature and he can't help it. He was delighted that his current wife Maria was already pregnant, and he so loved the thought of having another daughter to cherish. And ultimately leave.

Anyway, after his pile of pathetic excuses I told him about Dippit and her pregnancy problems. He was so concerned about Dippit. I was really surprised, but his reaction seemed genuine enough. Whilst travelling around the world, and being a total tart, he'd heard of something similar. He thinks it could be the combination of Dippit and Stan's essences so we should try to rebalance that. He was really quite hopeful and gave us a recipe to try. It goes...

One part Trifolium Repens picked during a full moon then soaked for three days in spring water. The spring must be located on one of the Greek Islands as Dippit is half Greek.

Four parts Trifolium Dubium picked during dappled sunlight then soaked in Irish whiskey. Not Scottish whisky. He was really specific about that too.

A measure of roasted barley.

A measure of hops.

A measure of roasted malt.

A pinch of yeast.

We think it could be a bread of some sort. Here's the note with the exact quantities of hops, malt and barley. It tells you how to cook it and how to prescribe it." Harry nodded and handed over the recipe.

Stan looked at the recipe, shook his head and then laughed. *"I know exactly what that is, and I can assure you that it's not bread. No, not bread at all, I say. Clever old Roger. I say, clever old Roger. I'll be back in twenty minutes. Twenty minutes tops. Gab, can you get off Fachance's knee? It is her knee? Then please give me a lift? A lift, please."* Stan was back to his repeating, so it was clear that he was also back to his contented self. He and Gab left in order to collect the mystery items. Fachance began eating the blanket.

"Anyway, after a few home truths and a couple of pokes to the

ribs, I can only hope that Roger learned his lesson. He promised to mend his promiscuous ways or use birth control. Wait. No, no, no. Willing. Do you know Willing?" Harry looked around the room.

"Yes, I know Willing. Your sister? She doesn't have wombats either. Just in case that was a thing now," Karen quickly reassured the panicked Harry.

"Thank goodness. I didn't realise until now what that could have meant. How that promise could have cost us Willing's very existence. Oh well, the aging Casanova didn't learn his lesson afterall. Just as well," Harry shrugged and accepted the hug from Karen. Karen also sneaked Harry a wee selection box. Well the finger of fudge from the selection box as no one's that keen on that chocolate bar, so it always gets left until the very last. Or eaten first to get it over with. Maybe there should be a study about how people eat a selection box and what it says about their personality. Bowie, step away from the puppies and get your thinking cap on

CHAPTER THIRTY-SIX

A few days later...

"*Yee ha!*" and Bub was violently driven backwards onto the floor. A forearm across his throat was closing his airways and ensuring that his breath was coming in short, painful gasps. He struggled to dislodge the determined, demented lump then gave up and cuddled her instead.

"*Harry, I've missed you, but it's only been a day or two. I didn't expect such a potentially death inducing welcome home. How are you doing my beautiful bride?*" Bub was still on the floor and thoroughly enjoying the warm, squirming female in his arms. Now that he could breathe, that is.

"*Ohhh I like the 'bride' comment, my groomy woomy. No, no that doesn't work for me. Yuck, yuck.*" Harry began to scrape her tongue and gag.

"*Eh, no it doesn't work for me either. So why the warm, choking welcome? Not that I'm complaining but it's been such a short separation, my bride.*" Bub smiled and pinged Harry's bra strap.

"*Ohhh, I'm never going to get enough of that pet name. Ahh, well. We've had a busy old time of it, and I could have done with your help. You gorgeous chuncka change,*" and with that Bub and Harry caught up on their most recent adventures.

One update later...

"*So the King and his brother are definitely unable to escape? The Crabs are happy and gainfully employed in Hell three. And the Knights have ignored Devil Keith's voting regime? Thank goodness for that. Those poor rabbit amputees. I wasn't sure if they'd need wheelchairs or pogo sticks.*

It sounds like a productive visit. Well done my Moonlight. No, no. No matter how many times I say it, that one doesn't work either." Another tongue scrape.

"Just stick with 'my majestic master' and we'll be fine. No tickling. No Tickling. No fair, my bride.

I thought Devil Keith would have done better in Florence. He's been doing really well recently. Suspiciously well... now that I think about it. I haven't had to rescue him from the wood nymphs for a few weeks. That was getting increasingly tricky. And before you ask. That's a story for another time, my bride." Bub assertively stated, then ruined his assertion by sticking out his tongue.

"Ok, we'll stick a pin in it, Doll-face. Doll-face, is that a maybe? Well about the Devil Keith achievements thingy...

I pinched some of Gab's truth-telling washing-powder and laundered Devil Keith's smalls. By the way, they're not that small. The powder did the trick, and I was able to get the truth out of him. Seemingly, he's been sneaking into Stan and Dippit's room to cut off some of Stan's hair for some type of money-making venture. I doubled the amount of washing-powder in Devil Keith's smalls, but he still manged to keep quiet about his scheme. Despite all the itching and clawing around in his nether regions. I was well impressed.

Anyway, during one of his midnight raids Devil Keith got some of Stan's hair in his mouth. Devil Keith swallowed the hair and since then it's helped him become a tiny bit lucky. That's what's behind his uncanny successes in Hell number three. I knew there was something fishy going on there.

While we were in Florence the luck wore off, hence the juggling debacle. On a positive note, Stan's taken the whole thieving thing surprisingly well. He had thought he had an iron or vitamin deficiency as he thought his hair and nails were no longer growing. Yeah, Devil Keith had also been biting Stan's nails as he didn't want the damage his own gel nails. So Devil Keith's revelation has reduced some of Stan's worries." Harry sagely nodded.

"And Dippit? She is definitely better. No more worries?" Bub checked as he had been extremely worried about his petite and

cheeky sister-in-law.

"No worries. Thank goodness. The recipe from that old reprobate Roger did the trick. The shamrock, and four-leaf clover infused pint of Guiness fixed her right up. Stan's mam had been unwittingly eating the shamrock all of the time during her pregnancies and she drank the Guiness for extra iron. Not just a craving for common grass at all.

We all need to pay a wee bit more attention and ask the right questions from now on. It would save us a lot of worry and some very bizarre adventures. Can you tell how fed up I was with the old time travelling? Plus I missed you so very much." Harry pulled him in for a snog and a fumble.

Forty minutes later...

"So Gab and Fachance, they're an item? Really?" Bub enquired as he turned his jumper the right way round.

"Yep, that Angel is well and truly broken. No more gadding around the top of the Christmas tree for him." Harry giggled.

"Harry, I don't think he did that. But it would be as funny as fudge if he did. Talking of Christmas trees. I popped into check on Mac on the way home. She's in a bit of a state because she's being punished for interfering in inter-Hell politics. It's in the Brownies pamphlet and seemingly it's a complete no, no.

She's had two more Brownies added to her collection and they brought some props with them. The Brownies forest has been sprinkled with razorblade, decorated Christmas trees and the new Brownies are obsessed with them. Brownie Hollie keeps eating the sparkly glass baubles as she loves the blood red lipstick effect and Brownie Nicola keeps breaking into the gunpowder laden Christmas crackers in order to find blue-stoned rings. Luckily, cursing Brownie Kat and little Brownie Louise are managing the crisis by building bombproof bunkers and trying to talk Brownie Hollie into using cruelty free make-up products.

I think we need to get them, and Brownie Lesley, some custard to say thanks for helping us and Mac." Bub decided.

"I'll make it pink custard. Brownie Kat said it gives her 'good memies'. I think that means good memories. And Brownie Mirka deserves a wee treat as she's kept on the wagon despite Brownie Kirsty and Brownie Liz tempting her with some homemade moonshine." Harry nodded and raided her kitchen cabinets.

"Roberto? What's he up to? Have the ladies of the Inches lured him to a handbag making party?" Bub enquired when he realised that Harry had some cupboards attached to the wall to raid.

"Oh he's having a great time in the Falkirk canals. And he absolutely loves Karen. I think Karen's part bacon, as the Hounds of Hell are big fans too. Oh, there are two new litters and two of the puppies are gonna be adopted out to the Brownies. Olive and Rolly. They're adorable and really sweet on each other. I can't describe how happy that makes me feel. Happy and safe." Harry smiled, remembering them eating through their titanium chew toys.

"What a relief. Now this is total gossip, but also totally true." Bub mannishly giggled and whispered into Harry's ear. "The maintenance men told me that Karen has a secret room with a black, leather adult swing. I'm gonna buy her an ice-cream maker and ask for an invite to her play park."

"Bub, that might not go the way you expect it to. Not at all." Harry warned.

CHAPTER THIRTY-SEVEN

T hings are peachy...

Hell number one was back in business and everyone was upright. The *"guests"* had been moved on and they were happily reconfiguring Hell number three. The playful new puppies were with the Brownies and thanks to Brownie Hilary's forgiving ways, the threatening bricks were back to their original Faery crunching schemes.

Roberto, the crocodile, had permanently moved in to Camelon and was backstroking around the canals and visiting the Kelpies. His floral swimming caps and matching goggles were causing quite the stir with the locals.

Our lovely Dippit was vertical once more and back to her teasing and naughty little plans. The seven pints of herb infused Guiness had done the trick. That's seven pints per day, mind you. Stan had finished crocheting a travel cot so Aunty Harry and Uncle Bub can babysit when the wee cherub arrives. Aunty Harry was unravelling the crochet so that Mummy Dippit and Daddy Stan could keep the napping changing, winding and burping all to themselves. Afterall, no one had helped her potty train Devil Keith.

So in response to their recent successes the Hell number one team decided to throw a joint hen and stag *"do"* for all the newlyweds. A *"Shag Do"* as it was lovingly referred to. And a baby shower was wedged into the celebration as well, as Karen didn't want to lay on a second buffet for Fachance to demolish. Devil Keith also managed to squeeze a Halloween party and a Saint Patrick's Day float into the mix too.

So half of the Hell number one were team *"Halloween, Wedding and St Patrick's Day"* so they dressed accordingly as robotic, killer leprechauns with pots of keenly sharpened frisbees rather than pots of gold. Whilst the other half of Hell opted for the much more sensible *"Baby Shower, Wedding and Halloween Bleeding"* complete with baby-grows, bibs and dummies. Bibs with gnashing teeth and dripping in blood clots, but bibs none the less. Plus, dummies with concealed knives, poison capsules and mini fireworks finished the look. This is Hell afterall.

Following a particularly rowdy *"pin the tail on the donkey"*, or to be more precise, *"pin the sperm on the egg"* competition they decided to call it quits for the night. All the food was gone as well as the plates and the tables the food sat on. Fachance was picking her teeth with the remains of the chocolate fountain pump. The Falkirk sewers were no more, and Harry announced that they had to arrange a haggis hunt to replenish her supplies. The red paper hats were scrunched up in the rubbish bins and the goodie bags were triumphantly carried off to their respective homes and offices. They did so enjoy a wee yoyo or two. They weren't savages, afterall.

They had agreed on a day to recover from the party then they were off to search for the Big Bang Runes. They were all deeply concerned as they had no idea where to start this fantastical search. Luckily the Oracles had agreed to continue lending them the Time Scavenger so they could painstakingly search through time for the artifacts.

Harry and Bub's abode after the Shag Do...

An ever so slightly drunken Bub delicately dipped a finger in the pink custard then gently bopped Harry on the very tip of her freckled nose. Harry dipped two fingers in the custard and playfully swiped Bub's cheek and jaw. Bub stuck his hand in the pot of custard and pored a fist full of warm dessert on Harry's head. Harry picked up the pot of custard and lobbed it at Bub's chest. Therein started the great, pink custard war of 2023.

An hour later and the warring parties emerged from a hot, steaming shower and into a rather splattered, womb-like pink room.

"All this food on the walls is making me hungry. You?" Harry asked as she towel dried her hair.

"I could eat. You lost the fight. So go get some food, woman. Your man is starved and needs sustenance," Bub tapped Harry on her pert bottom then tugged on a clean shirt and went to attach his favourite black cufflinks. Harry growled then rugby tackled him onto the bed and started a tickle fest. There was an almighty bang and the room descended into utter, dense darkness. The temperature dropped dramatically, and the air became frigid. There was complete, unrelenting silence. A bright green, dazzling yellow and turquoise light flashed into being above their bed. The light was infused with small glittering stars and rapidly rotating planets, complete with bouncing moons and zipping comets. A deep, commanding voice rang out.

"When Bub finds the love of his life,
When Harry becomes his loving wife,
When they handfast, then touch lips,"

"Oh pretty... you'll find that they're mine. Give them back. I want my cufflinks back this minute." Shouted a petulant, childlike voice from the darkness.

"............................ Apocalypse. Tap Runes twice to repeat the prophesy." The voice politely instructed and the galaxies began to fade. Bub and Harry strained to see.

"Devil Keith is that you in the darkness? Where the fudge did you come from? We think we've accidentally found the Big Bang Runes, but you interrupted the prophesy. A fudging prophesy. I can still hear you. Are you licking the walls over there? You complete

twit." Bub didn't know whether to jump for joy, as they had found the Runes, or crack Devil Keith off the wall as they had missed a vital part of the prophesy.

"I heard about the custard and just knew you'd fight over it. You're just so childish. I came along to claim the spoils of war." Devil Keith traced his tongue over a particularly long drip of pink pudding.

"Just tap the Runes and you'll hear it again. Sheesh, let me do it. I have to do everything. 'Devil Keith, save us!' or 'Oh, master of red squirrels, save us!' That's all I hear. Day in, day out. It's exhausting. You have no idea just how exhausting." Devil Keith was making jazz hands then grabbed Bub and knocked his wrists together. The prophesy rang out again but the crucial words, just before the word Apocalypse, continued to be muffled and incoherent.

"Sorry you have exceeded the four-repeat limit," a less commanding and more nasally voice smugly informed them. The rainbow of lights continued to slowly dissipate, and the room came back into view.

"Should have used pigeons. I always say." Devil Keith sighed.

"What? Who carries pigeons around with them? They're basically flying rodents." Bub was gobsmacked by the bizarre suggestion.

"I do and I have 'a' recording. I always keep 'one' going. You never know when 'you'll' need it. And for your 'information': pigeons are nothing like frogs." Devil Keith gushed through his air quotes whilst wresting with a particularly reluctant dollop of dessert. He then promptly pulled a plump pigeon, by its throat, from his jacket pocket. He tapped its beak 32 and half times, to ensure the clarity of the recording. But the essential words, just before the word Apocalypse, continued to be lost to the ether.

"There's no other alternative. We have to go see the Oracles." Bub was exasperated by the development. He had a fresh batch of sticky toffee pudding in the oven.

"Not the fudging Oracles. Nothing good ever comes of visiting the Oracles. Devil Keith put your handbag back, you're not going Drill shopping again." Harry pulled on her socks and

THE DEVIL'S A HUNTING

CHAPTER THIRTY-EIGHT

O ff to the Oracles…

"We told you not to come back here until you had our Big Bang Runes. Be off with you, you peasants and do our bidding." The Oracles were cool to the point of being glacial towards Bub, Harry, and Devil Keith.

"These? You mean these?" Bub opened his hand and showed the cufflinks to the Oracles.

"Oh, ya dancer! Ya belter. Our stones! Our girls are back where they belong," and the Oracles began energetically jigging around the cluttered room. That was followed by a clumsy rendition of The Bump then Marjorie threw Gilbert into the air, caught him, and dipped him to the floor. They then decided they'd danced enough as Gilbert's ballet shoes were pinching his toes and he had a recital later.

After the curious dance moves the Oracles asked their *"saviours"* to ask them questions. Any question at all. The more complex the better, they prompted. Just this once, mind you, the Oracles would answer any question. No matter what. Carte blanche on the old questioning front. The Oracles then asked them to stop asking them questions after Devil Keith asked them *"Why?"*, fifty-two times. Just the word *"why"* followed by a mimed question mark and a sad face.

Harry was astounded at the changes in the Oracles. Their eyes were clearer and their whole demeaner was so sharp. So focused; even their posture had improved. There was a clarity that Harry had never thought she would ever see. Their dress sense hadn't changed but somehow Marjorie and Gilbert were rocking the matching caramel brown polyester slacks, clunky orthopaedic sandals (Gilbert had gratefully changed his shoes), and washed-out red polo shirts. They looked good. Like, good for their age, good. Well, middle-aged good. Paunchy, middle-aged spread... good.

"Now what can we do for you? You bright little things. You bringer of such delightful gifts." Gilbert pinched their cheeks then went in for a second wee pinch just to make sure they knew how truly clever they were.

Bub explained that they had found the Big Bang Runes by accident as they had *"knocked out"* a prophesy via his new cufflinks. Unfortunately it was an incomplete prophesy as Devil Keith had interrupted it mid-flow.

"Oh, not to worry. You get a couple of chances to repeat the prophesy. Just give them another tap and take some notes. That's what we normally do. I think." Another wee cheeky pinch was added to the team's collection. Harry was beginning to worry that Gilbert would suffer a repetitive strain injury.

Bub explained that they had tapped the cufflinks a second time then a third time, but the prophesy had told them that it was unable to provide another reading as they had used up all their chances.

"Yep, that happens. It's a failsafe so that prophesises can't be re-used or re-listened to by unscrupulous people. Hear that Marjorie? I knew why the Runes didn't work. I'm a total treasure." Gilbert grinned and pinched Marjorie's wobbly bottom. He was clearly in one of his rare pinching moods and Harry made a mental note to send him one of her many wrist splints.

"Ohhh, Gilbert we have company. Later, you studly stud. Oops, sorry. He's such a beast, I'll have you know. There was this time I bought some small, firm cabbages... Devil Keith if you're going to be sick use the rubber plant in the far corner. It could be doing with a

good feed. Harry, I'll tell you about the cabbages later. Take it from an old married lady...it's good to have a wee treat up your sleeve for an anniversary.

Anyway, tell us what you heard, and we'll see if we can patch it back together. We've probably heard it all before but forgotten." Marjorie nodded to Harry and pulled out her diary to organise a coffee date.

Bub and Harry told them what they heard and what part of the prophesy was missing. The Oracles also enquired about the location of the stones, the colours of the lights and how Bub had acquired the cufflinks. Bub explained that they had come into his possession after or possibly during the Eva/Karen incident. He couldn't fully recall that time and he wasn't too keen to try to remember it. Atlantis and veins!

"Humph. Understandable, lad. Well, your prophesy about meeting and marrying our Harry was complete so technically this one's not about you pair. You two are only used as a reference point.

So I think we can all agree that this prophesy is probably or maybe linked to the whole Devil Keith and Nora dating type thing. That's why you ran out of chances to repeat it. I'm sure I've heard something like it. However, I think Eva used you, Bub, to access the prophesy as technically it's usually only Marjorie and I that can do that.

In rare instances the person pertaining to the prophesy, or named in it, can also access the details. The most likely scenario is that Eva got to it first, heard it and then probably tampered with it to hide the evidence. I think she wanted to use it to distract Devil Keith while she carried out her terrible plan. What say you, Marjorie?" Gilbert was no longer sounding like a tanned-up gorgeous Aussie. He had reverted to his Yorkshire *"I have a load of sheep stuck in a well"* accent.

Marjorie agreed with Gilbert and suggested that the Apocalypse either will happen or won't happen depending on whether Devil Keith meets or doesn't meet Nora. They didn't have a clue what the missing words were. So basically they were no further forward on the whole *"end of the world"* Apocalypse thingy. Harry decided that she had over-estimated the Oracles new clarity. Marjorie also decided that they had put too much emphasis on the Runes and looked longingly at Ryan Reynolds grease-stained profile.

"Was my prophesy something similar?" Bub looked hopeful.

"No lad. Your prophesy was about malaria and quinine or marriage and quintuplets. There was definitely an M and a Q in it. We didn't want to tell you that we might have made a few errors in the interpretation when we listened to it, but we think we got the gist." The pizza box was looking increasingly inviting.

Devil Keith dug around in his pockets and rubbed his lips. *"We could try the pigeon again?"*

"It didn't work the last time so why should it be any better now?" Bub questioned.

"Oh, it just might." And Devil Keith wiped a speck of dust from his lip glossed pout.

"Do you happen to have some of Stan's powdered nail clippings with you?" Harry looked expectantly.

Devil Keith did have the nail clippings and yes, they did work a treat. They had the complete prophesy, and it was a doozey.

CHAPTER THIRTY-NINE

Somewhere in Falkirk...

"Hey, Scottish guy. Where would one find the delectable, Scottish Nora? She appears to have moved without informing me, her luscious lover, where she now resides. The naughty wee Mousetrap." Devil Keith was rubbish at pet names too, but at least he didn't refer to Nora as *"Bucket-features"*. Unlike one of the recently bruised authors.

"Just because I'm Scottish you presume I'll know all the Scottish women? Just give me a name and I'll perform miracles or conjuring tricks? Dance monkey, dance! Eh?" The Scottish Guy was waving his hands and wiggling his bottom in the air.

"Yes. Yes, I do. So, back to my delicious Nora. She's small, with an infected knee, a randy cat, flat feet, and she has the silhouette of a Christmas pudding? Not keen on Taxidermized flamingos either." Devil Keith buffed his nails and straightened his plum bow tie.

"Oh, that Nora. Up the road and past the Co-op. You can't miss her. If you see the resentful lollipop man then you've gone too far. Good luck, pal." Scottish guy waved and whistled as he daundered off to the bookies.

Devil Keith went past the co-op, then about turned so he could buy himself a limited edition caramel Wispa. He then found his Nora. His baby momma. His future happiness. His everything. She promptly and accidentally shut the door in his face then hollered something or other about a restraining order or calling the police or having him slung in gaol. Blah, blah, blah. Devil Keith wasn't really listening as he was entranced by her gorilla garden ornaments. Really should contact Grant, I need my wok back, Devil Keith mentally noted.

After thirty minutes of screaming through the letterbox Stan appeared with the loved-up Gab and asked Nora to let him and Devil Keith in. Devil Keith had a lot of explaining to do and he needed to put a particularly fetching plastic gorilla back where it belonged. Beside Nora's garden pond...in Scotland... fishing. Yep, that's realistic and where you would normally find gorillas. Straight off the pages of the August edition of the National Geographic.

Two hours later...

*"So we've been on many dates? Not just the date to the cinema where you nearly bored the tits off me? That was the date where I met Stan. I really know you, like **really** know you? Not just as the guy who won't stop hanging around my gate with a bloody big and threatening wrench? The guy I went to court to get rid of? The restraining order guy?*

You changed the whole world's timeline so you could woo me or, to be correct, so that I would forget you and your sorry ass wooing?

You're also the reason that my optician had to nail in my contact lenses? He nailed them with carpet tacks then said that if that didn't work he'd have to use 3-inch galvanised nails to keep them from slithering out. Great big nails in my eyes!

You're the reason I can't go to the Cat Café or the Kelpies without adult supervision or a signed note from my mum. No one, not even the servers, knew why I was banned but they were adamant that I produced the note or my mum holding my birth certificate. Unbelievable. Just unbelievable." Nora threw her hands in the air and went to leave the room. She then turned back because it was her bloody house and that kaftan wearing moron was leaving.

*"Yes, I am. I am **he**. So 'glad' you finally noticed. So now we've cleared all that up... 'how' about it? Ready 'to' get horizontal, fertile*

and push out my babe? Eh? Ready for 'a' wee Devil Keithie cuddle. Wink, wink." Devil Keith beckoned Nora over to sit on his lap.

"Give me a minute while I consider your highly flattering and romantic offer. **No.** *That will be a firm* **no.** *Now take your red fluffy mules and trip back out that door."* As soon as the words left Nora's mouth she realised that Devil Keith didn't understand sarcasm and he also seemed to be struggling with the concept of air quotes.

"You don't understand. The fate 'of' the world rests 'in' your ample hips." Devil Keith courageously went in for a full body hug.

"It's 'on' my hips. And no it bloody well doesn't. Stan, remove that sorry excuse for a man or he can pick his window. He's leaving." Nora picked up the empty Wispa wrapper and stuffed it down Devil Keith's top. She just couldn't be doing with this. She had her windows to clean.

Stan stepped in to calm the situation. How were they going to save the world when Nora hated Devil Keith? Plus her hatred was completely justified. Stan was just hearing the extent of Devil Keith's previous wooing attempts and he was appalled by all of it. Stan, you should have read book one. Then you wouldn't have been so keen to be in the other books, whispered the authors.

Two minutes later…

"Say that last line of the prophesy again." Sighed Nora. Pushing the horny Hercules off her knee. She really needed the opposite of Viagra. Argaiv, maybe?

"It goes. 'Nora might save the world with love from Mr Apocalypse'. Pretty serious stuff. You should be honoured and kissing my recently moisturised feet." Devil Keith put his feet on Nora's coffee table and emphatically nodded.

"Wait. Wait. This makes no sense. Why would Eva send you to me in the first place? She encouraged you to pursue me. Actually, she went further than that. She told you I'd give you a child. And… your name is Devil Keith Apocalypse? Really?" Nora wasn't sure

whether she should laugh or have him assessed by a mental health service.

"We think. I say, we think that Eva knew about you and tried to tamper with the prophesy. I say, the prophesy. But she didn't know who Mr Apocalypse was. Who he was. She never would have ever, ever, ever considered it was Devil Keith. Never Devil Keith, I say.

We think her aim was to keep Devil Keith busy during her take-over of Hell number one. Number one, I say. Adding the bit in the lavender note about you being Devil Keith's babby momma was to try to keep him focused and motivated. Keep him motivated, I say. That would keep Harry busy too, saving Devil Keith. I say, saving Devil Keith. Eva probably thought Devil Keith would break you, I say break you. So stopping the whole prophesy in its tracks. The prophesy, I say." Stan made some good points, so Devil Keith decided not to correct him about the whole *"Harry saving Devil Keith"* myth. He had no idea where that came from or who started it. Devil Keith decided that after the whole Nora birthing his exemplary sprog he would launch an investigation on an episode of *"Myth Busters"*.

"Yes I changed my name by Deed-poll a couple of weeks ago. D'Evil sounded like I was an out and out baddie, and it was negatively affecting my swipes on Tinder. However it was positively received on Grinder. Oh yeah.

And it's Devil Keith Mr-Hyphenated-Apocalypse. So if you're lucky enough to win me over you would be. Drum roll, please. Mrs Nora Mr-Hyphenated-Apocalypse." Devil Keith beamed then bowed to an invisible but wildly ecstatic audience.

"Well that's settled it. Nope. Get out." Nora hollered and picked up her bottle of Windolene.

CHAPTER FORTY

Still in Falkirk…

"*Stan, the scissors, please. I can't believe I've been reduced to begging. I'm a catch. When will the little Mousetrap understand and be suitably appreciative?*" Devil Keith held out his manicured hand.

"*Nope. No, I say. Bub said no trickery this time. No tricks. No hair or nails, I say. You have to do this on your own or the prophesy will go off. Go off, I say. Or do something strange. I say, do something strange. Step back from the scissors. The scissors, I say.*" Stan wrestled the scissors from Devil Keith's grasp. They were making quite the scene outside Nora's semi-detached house.

"*Stan, I can't do this on my own. She's so unreasonable and short-sighted and just basically short. I think she's an inch off technically being classified as a midget.*" Devil Keith shouted and the lollypop man laughed.

"*She's also still here and I'm short-sighted because you wrecked my vision with all the whirling.*" Nora always did the outside of her windows before the insides.

"*Ah, I thought that because it was a new chapter you'd be somewhere else. My bad.*" Devil Keith winked and pointed out a smudge on the glass.

"*This is my house and my street, so you need to be somewhere else. New chapter? What are you blether on about man?*" Nora was angrily dusting her plastic gorillas and checking their fishing lines for bait.

Stan talked Nora into letting them back in her house as

the lollypop man was heading over to join in the debate. He also agreed to re-wire her sockets so they would shout *"I'm free"*, whenever she needed a spare socket to charge her phone.

"Can you two possibly compromise? Compromise, I say. Devil Keith's making a bit of a pig's ear of it. A pig's ear, I say. But the prophesy is real and so is the danger. The danger, I say. Nora, can you try one date. Just one date, I say. Please." Stan pleaded.

"Stan, I believe you and much as I don't want to… I'll do this for you. Only because you look so stressed and upset. Oh, I meant to say, I'm so glad Dippit's feeling better. The herby Guiness fair did the trick.

But I have some demands. I want a date with some sea air and a bit of sand. I want real food with no mention of the age of the animal or its juices. I can't believe you told me about your Life Cycle Theory and thought it was a real chat-up line. The lollypop man was intrigued.

Live animals would be good but not essential. No subtitles and no taxidermy. A little bit of excitement would be good. Just a little bit, mind you. So not the cinema or the zoo, and not a specialist cafe. I don't want to be banned from somewhere I like, and I'd hope to go back to someday. But I still want a proper date. A planned, organised date where you have to behave like a gentleman." Nora was now polishing her glass clown collection. She so enjoyed a rummage in the charity shops and the treasures she collected.

"I want ten dates. You're obstinate and will need time to adjust to my magnificence. That's my first and final offer." Devil Keith crossed his arms and frowned at the clowns. How dare Nora rub males in front of me, he fumed.

"Five dates and you'll consider yourself lucky." Nora counter offered.

"Alright. Three dates it is, but I get to wear my vajazzelled capri pants." Devil Keith winked and pointed at his groin.

"Three dates and if you so much as look as if you're thinking about rhinestones I get to kick you in the nuts." Nora asserted.

"Oh you minxy, midget. Now I remember why I like you some much." Devil Keith winked and kicked over a smug clown.

Devil Keith whispered to a couple of cockroaches and promptly zoomed off. He returned fifteen minutes with carrier bag clutched in his hand. He grabbed the reluctant Nora...

CHAPTER FORTY-ONE

The date…

"*We're all going to die. We're going to be eaten alive. Don't just stand there like an idiot. Help me! Kick them. Kick them all.*" Nora leapt into Devil Keith's arms and wound her legs round his slim waist. She then tried to crawl up his body and over his head to get away from the gliding grey fins.

Devil Keith had fulfilled some of Nora's demands: there was sea, some sand, live animals, excitement, and real food on the date. He may have taken some of her demands a little too far as he had chummed the waters with the very best stewing steak from the butcher's, Patrick's of Camelon. Consequently they were now surrounded by great white sharks. Sharks that had enjoyed the butcher's finest and were now planning on supplementing their daily roughage intake with surfboard. The red and black surfboard that had, until very recently, been under Nora's leaping flat feet.

"*You're half right and seventy-two percent wrong. You would have been eaten and died horribly but I, on the other hand, would have gotten a rather glorious suntan.*" Devil Keith was quietly smug until he looked at Nora. He quickly became exasperated and called on the nearest squad of snorkelling cockroaches. He then plonked the gasping Nora on the sandy beach.

"*Ready for 'a' snog my fulfilled Squeeze? My Mind-blown Midget? 'My' Flat-footed Femme Fatal? It would be easier 'to' indulge in a bit of the horizontal shuffle if you'd stop hanging off my hair and screaming 'in' my lughole. I don't want to have to 'put' you off because I have a headache. I know how to treat my dates and you my*

Stout Strumpet have been well and truly treated." Devil Keith was delighted by his ingenuity and was already considering rolling out his second-best beach towel. Ready for some lovin'.

Nora slid off Devil Keith and onto her knees. Gasping for breath and violently shaking she looked up at the hooligan. *"That wasn't a date. That was a slice of pure torture. That wasn't excitement, that was terror. Unmitigated terror. Take me home you bollocking buffoon and never contact me again."*

Nora's house and a pacing Stan...

Nora explained what had happened and Stan could see why she wasn't keen on any more of Devil Keith's outings. He ever so gently pointed out that Devil Keith had, technically, met her demands even if they were a bit extreme. Nora scowled so Stan changed that to very extreme. He also, timidly, reminded Nora that the fate of the whole world rested in her hands. Then quickly added that Dippit wouldn't be happy if he was sent home with vital parts of his anatomy missing or oozing.

Nora looked Devil Keith up and down. *"I can't believe I'm saying this. Do better next time. It's your last chance. No, don't try to negotiate. Come back tomorrow and bring me a bloody Wispa."*

Stan quickly explained that there was no need for actual blood on the Wispa. Or tissue. Or tendons.

CHAPTER FORTY-TWO

*D*ate 2.0...

"*You were snoring.*" Devil Keith said with wonder and a wee touch of anger.

"*Too bloody right I was. A date at a walking stick museum? What were you thinking?*" Nora countered and wiped drool from her chin.

"*I'll have you know that it was recommended by my dearest friend and sort of sister-in-lawish thing, Harry. Well she's less of a friend and more of a hanger-on. An unwelcome groupie... A polyp. A mop headed polyp. I think she'd agree with that. You've met her. You must agree that I've described her to a 'T'.*

Since you're still here... why are you still here? Anyway, back to you and this dating malarky. I was thinking that the museum met your unrealistically high demands. It was less exciting than the beach, and I didn't think you'd ever want to go back there so you wouldn't mind being banned." Devil Keith gave up counting on his fingers and considered using his toes.

"*Well you got that right, and this is my house. Of course I'd still be here.*" Nora was seriously considering throwing one of her least favourite figurines at Devil Keith, but she couldn't let Sylvia go.

"*To be honest I'm fed up with all your moaning. And the screaming. And the sexy swearing. Although that was quite stirring. And the pointing out of my flaws. I didn't think you'd be able to come up with one single thing that was less than perfect. Never mind the two pages of A4 you produced. It's the only reason that I'm giving you another chance. Under all that nylon and static you must have some hidden depths. Anyway, as you're soooo clever. I'm being sarcastic just in case your depths aren't really all that deep. Right, you pick the date and I'll attend. See how easy you find it, impressing a Supreme Being and all."* Devil Keith crossed his arms and pointedly stared at Nora. He had already given her fourteen of his business cards so she could address him appropriately. She had given all of the cards to her fire so she could warm her bum in front of the flames... appropriately.

Date 3.0...

"Ohhhh, niceeee one. I likeee. Maybe you do have a smidgen of a depth about you. Although it's well hidden." Devil Keith squealed.

"Thought you'd like it." Nora was feeling pretty smug. She'd cashed in her air miles, dragged Devil Keith out of Duty Free and they were currently standing in the Louvre gazing at the painting of the Mona Lisa.

"I would have loved to have seen his studio. The smell of his paints. Asked him about his inspirations. It was such a romantic time. I think I would have liked it there." Nora sighed and began walking to the next painting.

Devil Keith looked around him then whistled. Out popped a holidaying cockroach, complete with camera, battered flask, trail-mix, and map of the Paris underground. Devil Keith whispered in his ear and the cockroach sped away.

CHAPTER FORTY-THREE

Sometime later… in Hell number one…

"Has Nora always looked like the Mona Lisa?" Bub puzzled.

"A better question is: has the Mona Lisa always looked like my wifey, Nora?" and with that gem, Devil Keith slipped a rather large hacksaw into his back pocket.

The end

No, no, no. Finish the story before you have your roasted cheese on toast, shouted one of the proof-readers. Bloody amateurs. No wonder you've earned less than £30 from your first two books.

Ever so slightly later in Hell…

Devil Keith explained that Harry had evilly and wickedly stolen the Time Scavenger from Gab. Well, Gab had forgotten to put on the saw-shield, so the Time Scavenger had slowly ripped through Gab's cloak pocket. Devil Keith had double stitched that pocket so had written a letter to the thread manufacture about their shoddy product. Harry chose not to tell Angel Boy of her find and pocketed the handy device. All in all that was a good thing considering Gab's sulking and running away. And Harry's moaning about wrecking the timeline and all that balderdash.

Devil Keith kept rolling his eyes and miming shooting himself in the head.

When they all returned to Hell number one, and before the Runes' prophesy, Devil Keith purely and utterly accidentally acquired the Time Scavenger from the locked Safe. He was so gilding the truth. Devil Keith knew it and Bub certainly knew it, but Bub so wanted to know where this strange tale was heading.

In reality, Devil Keith had told Fachance there was a warm and gooey plum pudding in the Safe, so she had quickly eaten through the steel door to reach the treat. Devil Keith then helped to liberate the Scavenger from its exile. Not the scavenger Fachance, just to be clear. He told Bub that the tool was lonely and needed some company. More half-ish truths but Bub was impressed with Devil Keith's current thought processes.

So when his beautiful Nora wanted to see Leonardo's studio he felt obliged to help. She had had so many disadvantages in her short, podgy life so he decided to whisk her away and fulfil her wishes. Nora was stunned, excited and ever so grateful. Not grateful enough to kiss him or do any naughty things but there was a slight thawing, and she was less menacing towards his millinery projects.

Leonardo was mesmerised by Nora's feisty ways and diabolical threats to Devil Keith's person so Leo asked her what he could do for her. Nora chose to sit for the enigmatic Mona Lisa portrait. It also helped her cause that she adored the wombats, and she wasn't afraid of their cubed poo. Nora was desolate as she later found out that the wombats had been removed from her wonderful painting. Fachance and her bloody nibbling.

"*So my nearly normal Nora is famous. All thanks to little old me.*" Devil Keith crowed.

"*There must be more to this story. There's no way that changed her feelings towards you. Just no way. It would take sooooo much more than that. So much more for her to agree to marry you. I've met her and she's not a lunatic.*" Harry was adamant that there was more to the tale.

"*Let me continue, you hairy harridan.*" Devil Keith moaned.

Some truth...for a change...

From there Devil Keith had catapulted his Nora through time. They had changed the original drawings of the Eiffel Tower in the Champs de Mars, Paris. Altering it from being calculated in inches into being calculated in feet and yards. They had also increased the order for steel girders and rivets. Hence saving the striking landmark from its original design... looking like a desk tidy in to being the centre piece of the 1889 World's Fair exhibition. They had also shaved off Gustave Eiffel's moustache when he refused to add their names to the seventy-two other names etched on the tower. He told them that as they weren't engineers, scientists, or mathematicians they didn't deserve the recognition. Since then Nora and Devil Keith have tried to destroy the building by rusting it up, but the regular application of sixty gallons of paint just keep getting in their way.

"Still not enough. Remember I was with you in Falkirk, and I know you wrecked the Kelpies for her." Harry smugly announced.

"Tell her, Bub. Tell her to stop interrupting my chapter. This is my story. Mine." Devil Keith harrumphed.

Some more truth...for a change...

Nora had wanted a bit of sun. So Devil Keith and Nora visited Spain. 218 BC Spain, that is. Where they met Hannibal Barca, the famous Carthaginian General. More famous than his brother-in-law. You know, the handsome one of the pair.

The General was hell bent on having a final punch-up with the interfering Romans. He'd already gone a good couple of rounds and was raring to go again. During a night of some jolly good tequila Nora and Devil Keith had managed to talk him out of using horses and mules in his fight against the Roman legions. They had suggested helicopters and tanks to the puzzled soldier, but for the tipsy life of them they couldn't remember who made them during that time frame. After a bit of spit balling and lemony humous, Devil Keith and Nora had suggested that North African war elephants would be the dog's bollocks. They were bigger and nastier than their Indian cousins but worth all the extra trampling and tusk goring.

The following day Nora and Devil Keith had left the camp with an extra-large bag of peanuts, a couple of beach towels and a bunch of hair nets. They tempted the nut addicted war elephants across the rivers and forests into the General's camp. They then helped to train the bad-tempered pachyderms by offering them warm bubble baths, lip balms, and shea butter wraps. The happy, and well moisturised, elephants were essential in Hannibal's trek across the Alps into the Italian peninsula and the subsequent defeat of the Roman forces. Following the victory Hannibal was the talk of the town as he kept his elephant, Surus, as a well-loved pet rather than roasting him with crushed basil, parsnips, and diced onions.

Back in Hell...

Bub told Devil Keith that the victorious battle had always been the case. That it was well documented in all the history books, but Devil Keith just tapped his nose and said, *"of course it was, wink, wink".*

"Here's some beads from our latest holiday. They're just for you, Bub. Harry, you'd look totally preposterous wearing them. People would just think they were more of your bumpy, pimply skin. But blue instead of your usual inflamed red and pusy yellow.

So, let me continue my story, you gravel skinned Harpy." Devil Keith stated then dodged a punch.

Some more, more truth...for a change...

After Africa, Nora had told Devil Keith that she'd always wanted to see Las Vegas. Devil Keith got it a little bit wrong, but stowing aboard one of Christopher Columbus' boats and helping him in his discovery of the Americas had been one of the highlights of their adventures. Chris' *"discovery"* just happened to be on the same day that Nora and Devil Keith had indulged in a rather fractious game of *"hide and seek"*. Nora may have knocked off the steering and they turned right instead of left or left instead of right. Devil Keith had assured her that the East Indies were just around the corner and if need be, Chris would just bump into the West Indies instead. Devil Keith said Chris was gonna turn a profit no matter where he landed, so told her not to worry.

It was on that day that Nora looked at Devil Keith, without gagging and vomiting. She realised that she might kinda like him. She also became aware that the more time she spent with Devil Keith the more she admired him, or to be more precise the more time he had to wear down her resistance. Devil Keith insisting that America should be re-named Norca, in her honour, had pretty much sealed the deal. She refused the offer as it sounded weird. Keica sounded so much better, but after contacting Karen for permission she had vetoed both suggestions.

Back in Hell…

"So I slipped on the ring and fulfilled the prophesy. There you have it. Your brother has been hogtied. Good and proper." Devil Keith grinned.

"You also love her. Saving the world wouldn't have been enough of an incentive for you to tie the knot. Bro." Bub correctly guessed.

"Well she is pretty special, in a Christmas pudding sort of way." Devil Keith was hiding his rapidly reddening cheeks but there was no getting away from it. The Devil was no longer courting and very happy about it.

Bub wondered when Devil Keith would realise how alike Harry and Nora truly were. Bring on the screaming.

CHAPTER FORTY-FOUR

F inal update...for now...

Willing and Cesealia are travelling the world looking for the Selkie's fur coat. The fact that the searchers are conducting their mission whilst based on a luxury yacht is neither here nor there. Nor is the fact that all the crew are topless. Even when cruising the Artic there are nil shirts on board. The sailors' protruding nipples are proving to be handy for Willing to hang her coat off.

Dippit's pregnancy cravings have really picked up now that she's conscious but always slightly drunk. She's currently craving pickled onions, marmite on toast, fried leeks and bags of Seville oranges. She's paying for this as she has chronic heartburn and has a brown paper bag containing a bottle of Gaviscon with her at all times. She's been stopped a few times for vagrancy due to the dodgy paper bag activity and theft due to the stealing of the antiacids. However, the local constabulary ran out of notebooks due to Stan's repetition, so all charges were dropped.

Dippit also sniffs the odd fence. Creosote is wonderfully fragrant and not at all a crime. Stan is having sympathy cravings. He's working his way through his second field of tulip bulbs and the Netherlands have added him to Interpol's most wanted. He's currently seventh on the Red List and the midwife is not a fan.

The hot tempered Fachance was so annoyed to find the empty Safe that she pinched or stole (tomato, tomahto) the Time Scavenger from Devil Keith when he returned from the Americas. Gab and Fachance are curtly introducing Karaoke and a *"pie and a pint"* to the Renaissance period. It's proving very lucrative.

Wee Liam and Patrick are still grounded but they're well on their way to constructing their own trans-dimensional transporter so they can visit Winnie the Pooh and cheer up poor, depressed Eeyore. They had saved up all of their Christmas cracker jokes in preparation for their caring adventure. They just need their dad to use more toilet roll so they can get the necessary cardboard tubes. The wee scones...ahhh.

Ohh, not quite so sweet afterall. They appear to have found out about the power of Senna and so has their poor, loose bowelled father.

Dr Riel just discovered that Karen's varicose veins are a long lost treasure map. They've given up on the adult swing idea and are off to search for the Lost City of Atlantis. First stop, Corfu and a beach barbeque. Then a wet tee-shirt competition. Karen's already sunk their budget, betting on Dr Riel winning the contest.

Little Brownie Lesley has left Hell number two and has set up a jewellery shop next to a dentist's surgery. It ensures that she has a ready supply of fresh teeth. Devil Keith is pleased as he felt the regular concussions and extractions were impacting on his Mensa membership.

Brownie Rachel has also left Hell number two and is currently under contract to Ru Paul's Drag Race. She's a dab hand with the electric rollers, hair removal and chiffon scarves. Trevor joined her. He does a mighty good version of *"I will survive"* by Gloria Gaynor, but it might not save him from next week's elimination round.

Nora found out about Devil Keith's hair obsession and his money-making venture. She so approves and has bought shares in the dastardly scheme. They're going to be rich. Just as well as they've just been billed for turning Stonehenge into a destination wedding venue.

Bowie continues to wander around Hell. She is now fluid in Spanish but needs to wash her hair and she would benefit from a twelve-step programme to help her deal with her addiction to peey tea. As an aside…someone really needs to buy a visitor's book and have an up-to-date fire list. Anyone could turn Hell number one into their permanent home. Anyone.

After all the trauma Harry and Bub decided that they deserved a honeymoon. Venice has sunk another ten inches and neither of them are willing to say what happened.

So everyone is content and living their best life away from the humdrum daily toil of Hell number one. Hope someone remembered to turn the answering machine on as Devil Keith and Nora's prophesy is still very much alive and the world is very much not saved.

CHAPTER FORTY-FIVE

A blackened finger scrapped then emerged from the primordial sludge. John O. Vox stopped. Vincent Blitzing was awake.

◆ ◆ ◆

BOOKS IN THIS SERIES

The Devil's a ...

The Devil's A Courting

The Devil's A Fighting

The Devil's A Hunting

The Devil's A Learning

Printed in Great Britain
by Amazon

38551758R00096